Fossegrim
Book Three in the
Undraland Series

By

Mary E. Twomey

DEDICATION

For Saxon Boaz-Danger Twomey

Buy your mother lots of presents.

One.
Adrift

Foss shook his head as he, Jamie and I ran away from the lake where the Nøkken portal to the Land of Be had just been destroyed by Nik. "We stick to the plan. Let's head for the docks. As soon as Alrik and Charles stop fiddling with the water, Tor will grab them and they'll meet us in Fossegrim." We were holding hands so Jamie could vanish us, which made for an awkward escape.

"What if they need our help?" I argued as we ran toward the ocean. Well, I ran. They trotted, their long legs making the trek far easier on them. "How can you be sure that bloody body we saw floating to the surface wasn't Jens?"

Jamie's steps faltered, but Foss righted him. Foss's response was firm. "Nøkken have the upper hand in a water fight. If we get involved, it'll mean death for us all. Those who can be of use are helping. We're sticking to the plan. Let's go."

I wanted to run back to Nik and Jens, but part of me saw the merit in Foss's logic. I wasn't even the best swimmer in gym class. And tritons? Those Nøkken were no joke. Plus, given my last experience when the Nøkkendalig attacked me underwater, I wasn't keen on getting back in a lake so soon.

Jens was probably fine. He had Uncle Rick, Charles, Britta and Tor. They would find him and help him. His body probably wasn't the one I saw with blood blooming out into the water in red puffs, streaking through the blue in ribbons. I felt cold and empty. The limbo of not knowing felt like a vice around my throat.

When we reached the dock, Foss took the lead. Jamie kept me vanished outside a small shanty just off the dock while Foss negotiated a small boat for us to cross the water in.

I had no idea Undraland was so vast. I heard Foss talking with the merchant, and he pointed to a piece of land so far away, it was barely visible. The dock worker had a fear of Foss that went beyond being intimidated by his physical appearance. Foss's reputation had preceded him. Whatever softening had happened as a result of Mace's whistle stripping away layers of his curse was pushed out by his sneer that seemed even more cruel than usual.

Foss paid the man, who began loading into the small boat the baskets Foss pointed to. There was a basket of food, one with blankets and clothes, one with nets, and a few I could not tell what was inside.

When Foss gave us a discreet nod, we made our way invisibly to the dock with quiet feet. Jamie lowered me down and Foss steadied me with his hands on my hips. I didn't love the fact that since I was the smallest of our trio, I was to sit on the floor between the two wooden seats. I curled my knees to my chest to make room for the invisible man.

The image of surely not Jens bleeding out in the water imprinted itself on the inside of my eyelids, taunting me whenever I drew breath. Since I was invisible and no one would see my miniature breakdown, I turned my head to the side and wept into Jamie's thigh.

Jamie ran his hands through my blonde tangles. "There, there. Nik knew this was a possibility. We all did going into it. There wasn't time for him to suffer much, and we must be grateful for that."

"Grateful? We have no idea if Jens is even alive! Nik's body surfaced, but Jens went down there invisible. If he's dead, will we even know? How will they find his body?"

Jamie gripped my hair too hard to be comforting. "When Tomten die, our magic leaves us, so he'll be easy to spot."

"That's it? That's all you can say? He's your best friend!"

Jamie didn't answer, but looked far off into the distance. Through the psychic bond we shared, I could tell he was not anxious to reach our destination, but more nervous for what happened when we did. "It's best we remain concealed in the land of the Fossegrimens. They don't value women as your culture does."

"Okay," I answered, forsaking open grieving and turning inward.

Jens could be dead right now. The invisible force I'd taken for granted was gone. I had hope that he would survive, but no assurances. I was more connected to Jamie than to him, and I really hated that. If he died, would I feel the ping? Would I know across an ocean in my heart that he stopped existing? Would the pounding in my chest feel hollow, or would I keep hoping for his return, eternally pining in my state of relationship limbo?

I was so tired of surviving. I rested against Jamie's thigh between his legs and closed my eyes, pretending the hand in my hair wasn't to vanish me, but to bring me comfort. I had to do a lot of pretending lately. I could feel Jamie's angst through our psychic bond, which only compounded my own.

Foss rowed us across the water toward the docks. As we got closer, the landscape changed. Instead of the vivid green of Nøkken with its gorgeous flowers and bursting nature, Fossegrim was only sparsely green with muted sand and limited foliage along the outskirts of the island. There were beige tents set up along the coastline with various merchants selling their wares. It was Aladdin's town from the cartoon I always thought was a little too racy to be for children.

Foss took charge, correctly sensing Jamie and I were useless in our current state. "You'll stay here. I'll send Viggo for you. He'll bring you to my house where we'll wait. Stay hidden until you get to my bedroom." He snapped his finger to make sure we were paying attention, since he couldn't see us. "Not my property. Not my house. My bedroom. If the Mouthpiece catches wind of you on Fossegrim soil, you'll be easy to find. He won't set foot on our land, but we don't want him to know that you have. The less people know you're here, the better. I have business to attend to, and then I'll be home."

Jamie agreed for the both of us, since Foss couldn't give a crap what I thought anyway. *Sure, let's split the group further. It's clearly proved a solid idea. Whatever. At least I get Jamie.*

Foss had rowed us for nearly three hours. I was just starting to get over my slight seasickness when we docked. "Lucy, where's your face?" Foss asked, reaching around near his knees.

"Right here," I said, hoping he could follow my voice and wouldn't have to pat me on the top of my head like a dog.

He did it anyway, and I cringed.

He bent his neck to try looking me in the eye. What he couldn't see was me obstinately looking toward the heavens. *Take that.*

"Look, rat. Jens and your world tolerate you better than I do or my people will. If you want to get out of this intact, you'll keep your mouth shut and your head down. You'll get a change of clothes from Viggo when you get to my house. Keep your head down like your maidenhood depends on it. They've never seen a blonde before."

"Don't talk about my virginity," I scolded, clutching tighter to Jamie's thigh. I took a breath and softened a little, since Foss was actually trying to be helpful. "But I can do that. Thanks for the heads up. No one ever tells me what to expect when we get to a new country."

His expression was a snarl, as it usually was. "I'm not doing it for you. I owe Jens more than he'll hold me to, and I don't like having debts. I'm keeping you safe for his sake."

"Aw, shucks. You say the sweetest things."

When Foss got out of the boat, it was like losing a

small elephant and a giant dark cloud. The boat floated at least a foot higher, and I felt like I could breathe well enough to feel the grief from leaving Jens and Nik behind.

Two.
Lost

The relief was short-lived. Not three minutes after Foss left us did a dockworker come to row the boat to a different port so an incoming vessel could dock.

Jamie panicked. "On my back," he instructed in a whisper.

I did not hesitate, since the worker's boot was coming right for my head. I wrapped my arms around Jamie's neck, and as the worker dropped down, Jamie hefted us onto the wooden dock. "Let's look for Foss," he suggested, letting me hop down so I could walk beside him. I clung to his hand to keep myself unseen.

I wanted to toss around the idea of just waiting by his boat, but what did I really know about finding someone while invisible?

We had to be careful when we moved through the fishermen as we made our way toward the traders to look for Foss. Trying to get people to not knock into you when you're invisible is tricky, especially with everything as packed as it was.

You would think locating a seven-foot tall mammoth of a man would be easy in even the thickest crowd, but apparently Foss only had a handful of inches on his peers. The Fossegrimens were a tall and surly bunch, all with matching sneers, darker skin and shifty black eyes.

"Hold tight to me," Jamie instructed, as if I needed to be told. I didn't want to be visible. Aside from the fact that I completely stood out with my jeans and lack of height, Foss had been right in his assessment of the view on women here. The few women that I saw were covered from head to toe and even wore a head-covering that shrouded everything but their face, which was pointed downward. They walked behind the men, never next to them. The very air I breathed had a tinge of dust and oppression mixed in that I could not help but be filled with.

Jamie moved from holding my hand to wrapping an arm around me, as if to shield me from harm. "I can feel your fear, *syster*. I'm here."

If I was to be stuck with someone for a lifetime, I could do a lot worse than Jamie, I decided.

"This was a bad idea," Jamie said, looking around at the many people who were not Foss. "We should go back to the docks and wait for anyone who comes looking for Foss's goods. This is too dangerous for you."

"Okay, yeah." I really hated being the handicap, but truth be told, I was terrified. This was a far cry from my comfort zone, and I just wanted out.

Jamie and I turned around to head back the way we came. We heard a horse-drawn cart coming our way, and Jamie ducked us inside one of the tented booths to sidestep it.

The stranger couldn't really be blamed. He couldn't see us. The man buying spices from the vendor did a wild hand gesture to match his "these prices are ridiculous" rant and clocked Jamie in the face, hurting us both. Jamie's head bobbed back and hit the tent pole at just the right angle. Dazed, he stumbled until he fell on the ground, taking me with him. His hand fell away from me before I lost consciousness, and all I could do was hope I was still somehow invisible to the natives.

Three.
Blonde in a Birdcage

I woke up to a headache so bad, I was afraid to open my eyes. Sure, there was a lump on the back of my cranium, but that wasn't why I was cringing. Jamie was far away, and the ache would last until he found me. The pressure was from more than just too much blood through constricted veins. My eyes felt bugged with the symphony of agony ringing behind my ocular cavities.

Hoping Jamie was awake enough to see through my eyes, I opened them to give him something to look at.

Bars. Metal bars greeted me like a punch in the face. I was in a cage built for one. It was like a birdcage on a concrete floor, but it was built for people. There were dozens of cages lined up in two neat rows with a walkway between them. The dim light filtered in through the barred narrow windows up by the ceiling. One woman per cage. A hostage for each container.

We were in a basement, otherwise known as a

dungeon. Some of the girls were still unconscious, thank goodness. They didn't want to see this. Others were weeping with a few crying out for their mothers. One woman called out for her head covering, and then I understood. The coverings were more of a protection than a punishment. None of the young women, really still girls some of them, had anything on their heads in here, whereas out in the market, you couldn't see a hair on their heads. My guess is it was either a shaming tactic inflicted upon them or a marketing technique to showcase what each of them had to offer.

Us. What each of *us* had to offer.

My head pounded in time with my heart, and I called out to Jamie in my mind to rattle him awake wherever he was.

The coherent women looked on me with relief, as if they didn't have to worry so much since there was blonde chum in the bait. Now I was wishing for a head covering.

The girl next to me looked no more than fifteen years old, and she was sobbing uncontrollably in her cage. I wished I could offer her comfort, but my skin was cold and clammy with terror. If I had comfort, I'd take some for myself.

Come on, Jamie.

I tried to look through his eyes, but there was only darkness. Though, it was hard to tell if I was really doing it. My head pounded so bad, I had a difficult time focusing.

There was a clanking of an old skeleton key in a door at the end of the dungeon. The warden, I'm guessing, escorted in a man who thought he was very important. Puffed out chest and change purse swinging to show off for the caged women, he sized the first few up as if shopping for a ripe tomato.

I tucked my hair into my shirt and dropped down into a ball, covering my head as best I could.

I lucked out, much to the misfortune of the woman whose screams would be embedded in my brain for the rest of my life. The man saw what he wanted in the first handful of cages, so he did not venture to me.

My head hurt so badly, it felt like it might split open at the seams. There was so much pressure behind my eyes; I was afraid of spontaneous blindness, if that was a thing. I'd never before had a fear of being sold into slavery, and the newness of my current reality painted me from the inside out with panic I was not equipped to cope with. I thought on the Buddhist monks that I'd read could change matter with their minds. I hunkered down in my little ball and ran thoughts of invisibility through my head. Over and over I tried to make my body nothing so it would not be seen by the next horrible man or the rats I could hear scurrying throughout the dungeon.

Innumerable hours passed, and I wondered if it was a good thing or a bad one to take a nap to try escaping my headache. Many of the girls were asleep, and those that were not were crying softly. I had no comfort to offer anyone. I actually felt pretty bad that our mission was to take away the Land of Be from them. It seemed like a fair option for someone who'd been through too much at the under-ripe ages I saw them at. To forfeit what was left of your soul for a lifetime of forgetting this awful day seemed like a bargain. To give up my right arm to keep hands off me felt like a good option.

I touched my sternum, searching for Linus.

The heart-shaped glass vial was gone. In my capture, someone had removed the necklace, taking my brother from me.

I sobbed as silently as I could. My brother was the only thing that was mine. He was supposed to go through life with me. My other half was probably being sold for a twenty and a pack of cigarettes.

Linus was gone, and I was alone.

I bawled into my hand, drowning in my fear and the pounding in my head I could not shake.

Four.
Aladdin's Ghetto

Someone stabbed at my ribs with a metal prod, jerking me awake too soon.

I felt my neck again, but Linus was still gone.

No, none of it was a dream. I was not in my bunk bed with Tonya. I would never see her again. There was no college, there was no family, and there was no Jens. Just a rough jab to my side that forced me to sit up to get away from it.

I looked up through my head-pained haze and saw pure malice looking down at me. Malice with money – not a good combination, given my current situation.

"She's not old enough to be useful on the fields or in the kitchen," the newcomer argued with the warden.

The warden was filthy, probably from spending his days abducting women off the streets in broad daylight. *Thanks, citizens who saw that happen and did nothing.* The warden was missing three front teeth. I was hoping it was from a woman fighting back and trying to knock some sense into him. His black hair was dry, brittle and torn clean out in parts.

The man considering my purchase looked at me with mild disdain and appraising interest. I slammed my will to be invisible over and over throughout my body, trying to make it the only thing in the air around me.

When that did not deter his gaze, it dawned on me that invisible might not be possible, but crazy sure was. I flipped a switch and became what I hoped looked like the most repulsive version of myself imaginable. I crossed one eye and started drooling big gobs of spit down my chin onto the floor. I reached out with my left arm, pretending my left hand was stuck in a shriveled, useless shape. I began singing the Partridge Family like it was my life's anthem, only I sang it in Spanish, which I assumed they didn't have here.

Thank you, David Cassidy. You saved my life. And thank you, Señora Brown, my sophomore Spanish teacher who translated one of my favorite songs for me. And let's face it, anyone who walks around singing the Partridge Family with such gusto for no reason is, well, probably crazy.

I slurred my words, so he would think something was wrong with my face or my mouth or my brain or whatever he needed to cross me off his list.

This only confused him. I wanted him gone. I grabbed the metal bars and slammed my forehead into them, smiling and laughing in my best insane villain voice. I cackled through the agony that knocking my already pounding head shuddered through me. The pain was so bad, it was only a matter of time until I finally bought a one-way ticket to Loonyland.

Stop, Lucy! You're going to knock us both out! I'm on a horse trying to find you! I can't fall down now.

I gusted out relief. "Jamie? Jamie?" I called aloud before realizing that would do him little good. I ignored the men before me and tried to communicate to him.

Where the smack have you been? I'm in Aladdin's ghetto over here, and you're gallivanting around on a horse! Get over here!

"Show me what else you've got. This one's been hit in the head too often. Shame. Golden hair like that..."

That's right, keep on walking.

Gallivanting? You only just woke up. I've been calling for you all night. Where are you?

I'm in a freaking dungeon, is where I am! I'm ten minutes away from being sold to some idiot with a nickel and a smile. Get over here and bring some money!

Where? Do you have any idea where they took you?

My heart sank. *No clue. Just follow your headache. If it gets worse, that's the wrong direction. Ride until your head doesn't hurt anymore. And hurry! I'm serious, Jamie. Don't let anyone buy me!* My heart broke afresh. *They took my necklace! I need it! Please, help me!*

There was a few minutes of silence, and then Jamie came back with, *Foss wants to know if there are men for sale, too, or if it's just women.*

Just women. A couple dozen of us. I'm in a freaking birdcage, Jamie! Ah!

I wasn't paying attention to my surroundings and found myself jerked out of the cage by rough hands.

Beady black eyes examined me, poring over my face and form to inspect for injuries. "Is her hair real? Not jinxed by some elf magic?"

"Real, sir. Just picked her up yesterday. Ripe for a bedslave."

That's what you think. I drooled on his hand and let my left eye go wonky. The man launched me back into the cage, where I smacked so hard against the bars, the only thing I heard was Jamie calling my name before we both went out like a light.

Five.
On Foss's Leash

When I blinked the world into focus, I was greeted with the same headache that threatened to drive me to insanity with its fervor. It was determined to take me down if Jamie and I were separated, and it was winning. Tor had mentioned people offing themselves who were laplanded. I was beginning to understand. If I actually lived past the next week, this would be a real problem that needed tackling.

Again I heard boots on the dirt floor, and the metal rod dragged against the bars on the cages, waking us all to the sound of our own worst fear realized. Women began weeping all over again. I wanted to join them, but I knew no one would listen to my tears. They heard crazy, so that was the language I spoke.

A slice of moldy bread was pushed through the bars, and a small dish of water. My stomach jumped on the food like an alien bursting out of my midsection.

Girls tackled their food like jackals, ripping apart the bread and devouring it in seconds. I eyed my dish with longing, but also with a note of healthy skepticism that had Tonya's voice laced through it. She would never drink something out of an unmarked, open container in a setting where it could be messed with. My mouth was dry and I was far weaker than I had been yesterday, but my resolve was still my own. I would not eat food from my captors. I would rather starve in a cage than be fed and live as a slave. They would carry my emaciated body out of here before I ate what slave traders gave me. It's not like I had a ton to live for. My family was gone and Jens was probably...

No. I couldn't say it, even to myself. If Jens was dead, I would wait until the last possible moment to feel that.

I broke my bread in two and passed it through the bars to the girls on either side of me. They had to really reach for it, but they took it with gratitude, devouring the crumbly bits in seconds.

The water was harder to resist, so I poured it out on the floor next to my cage so I would not be tempted later. I wrapped my arms around myself and huddled in the far corner of my birdcage. It wasn't quite the hug I was wishing for, but it did the trick of holding me together through the thrumming in my brain that was only slightly less intolerable.

Less?

Jamie? Jamie! My headache is getting less. You're moving in the right direction!

Lucy? Thank goodness. I gave up calling your name a while ago. Anything else you can tell me about your surroundings would be helpful.

I looked around for anything to report. *There's a*

tiny window near the ceiling, so we're in a basement somewhere. I can't see out the window, though. They're selling us off, Jamie. Please hurry!

We are, darling. Hold out as long as you can. We've been checking different traders all day. Foss has a few more he knows of.

A few more? What kind of awful place is this?

This is Fossegrim, Lucy. They've been given this island for a reason. None of us wanted to work with Foss, but their portal needs to be destroyed, too.

I'll bet the women make good use of the portal here. I hesitated before making my fragile opinion known to Jamie. The situation here is kinda all my worst fears doubled. Are you sure it's such a good thing to cut them off from The Land of Be here? There don't seem to be many solid options for women.

Jamie's answer was swift and laced with disgust and finality. Women are not granted access to Be in Fossegrim. Pesta would take them, but the men do not allow it. The portal is for people, and women are not people here.

You can guess how I feel about that. I rubbed my temples. You're getting colder. Turn around or something. It's starting to hurt more. I can't take much more of this, Jamie.

I'm riding a horse with this headache, Jamie answered back with a rare touch of irritation in his tone. If you could not knock us both out again, I would be grateful. I've fallen off this horse once. I don't look forward to doing that again.

Sorry about that. It's a little desperate down here. I didn't do that on purpose. They're not exactly careful *with the merchandise.*

Another set of boots entered the dungeon, inciting fear amongst the women. The weeping picked up, as did the praying and begging. I looked up at the man and shuddered. He had a giant scar down the length of his right cheek and walked with a limp. He was missing a tooth, which made his sinister smile all the more disgusting. He was bald, and his shiny head had sweat splattered across the tanned skin. He was easily seven feet tall and looked every bit the villain he was. He rattled around a brown sack of gold coins, sifting his fat fingers through them as he appraised each of us.

My headache started to lessen as he made his way toward my cage. I readied my drool, but since I was dehydrated, there was less of it at my disposal.

"This one," he ordered, jabbing his finger at my cage.

"Right away, Master Olaf."

Jamie, hurry! Don't let him take me! I gave Jamie a good fill of the man's face in case describing him to Foss would be helpful.

Terror lit my insides when the warden yanked me out of the cage, but I did not fight. I'd noticed the glee on the other buyers' faces when the women tried to get away. They relished a good fight, but they would not find one with me. I was limp and cross-eyed as the warden dragged me out by my long hair.

"I won't pay a full hundred for her. She's barely alive and not all there," the buyer argued. His breath stank like a landfill. "She's dressed like a man."

"But golden hair like the sun," the warden pointed out, yanking me to my feet and holding my hair up to the man to examine. "And you can dress her however it pleases you."

I cringed and tried to maintain my hold on appearing insane while both men smelled my dirty hair. Olaf's giant hand reached down and cupped my breast as I fought back the vomit and tears.

I screamed in my mind for my mom to comfort me, for my dad to save me, for Linus... just for Linus. I wished for death over and over, so I could be with my family and with Jens, who was most certainly dead. For if Jens were alive, this would not be happening.

Lucy! Lucy, we're here, I think. Foss is on his way in.

The bile built up inside of me the longer Olaf's hand rested where it was not welcome. I didn't mean to, but I couldn't hold back the puke. I vomited all over the man, soaking his shirt in my sick. I was almost a little bummed I didn't have more in my stomach to launch at him.

I was thrown roughly back into the cage, which I was beginning to find comfort in. The warden came by and dumped a bucket of water on me to clean me off. I shrieked at the freezing splash, but other than that, made no noise. I closed my eyes and shivered in the sliver of light let in through the tiny window. Another woman was chosen, and I took responsibility for her screams. She was a fighter, and it would cost her dearly.

I was a survivor, though I could not give myself a solid reason why. I think it was just that I didn't want to go out like that, at Olaf's awful hands. I tried to scrub the echoes of his touch off my body, but it stayed there.

As the handprints of the Nøkkendalig began to heal and fade from me, the Fossegrimens added theirs to my damaged psyche.

Before I realized what was happening, my cage was opened again, and I was dragged out by my hair once more and thrown onto the floor.

"A hundred for this piece of sewer water?"

My spirits lifted at the sound of Foss's voice. I raised my chin to look at him, and was greeted by the back of his hand. Hard and solid as the rest of his body, his hand sent me flying backward, knocking my body against my cage. Something cracked. I felt the change in my ribcage and cried out involuntarily. I couldn't tell if my rib had broken or if it was just badly bruised. Either way, when Foss yanked me up by my damp hair, my left side felt like it was on fire.

Foss sneered, "I'll give you sixty."

"The hair alone's worth more than that. Scalp her, and all your girls can be blondes," the warden suggested.

I covered my mouth with my hand to keep from crying. I didn't dare raise my head to look at Foss again.

Foss's gruff tone was firm. "I don't barter. You'll give her to me for sixty, and be grateful I do business with you at all."

The warden observed his damaged goods with a heavy sigh. "Alright. Sixty it is."

Foss shoved the money at the man and jerked me up. I remembered not to look at him this time and kept my aching ribs to myself.

My obedience wavered when a rope went around my neck. I started hyperventilating, which nearly crippled me with the ache in my ribs. I clawed at the rope, but it was already tightening uncomfortably around my throat. I gasped for air when Foss yanked on the tether. My feet moved on their own, following his large footsteps out of the dungeon and into the store above.

There was no scandal to a man leading me around like a dog. A few people gave me an appraising look because of my hair or my size, but no one stopped Foss. No one spoke on my behalf. They went about their normal bustle of life and did nothing to stop the cruelty.

The Nøkken turned a blind eye to the Nøkkendalig. The Fossegrimens accepted slave trading. Evil was rampant, and no one cared enough to lift a finger in protest.

Right then I vowed I would do whatever it took to destroy their portal. I would take away the blissful retirement from the men and force them to live with themselves until they died, old and decrepit with nothing but their bad choices to cling to.

I held my side and walked hunched over to give the tender area extra care. I stumbled when the full blast of midday sunlight hit me, and choked on the leash when Foss jerked it to keep me from misbehaving. I blinked to adjust my eyes to the light as I fumbled along behind Foss. He led me to two horses. One was for him, and the other I guessed held Jamie in his vanished form. I was shoved up on the horse with Jamie and tied to the flank. Jamie loosened the noose so we could both breathe a little easier and kissed my head. "It's alright. You're out of there. You're safe."

I had no response to this. Yes, I was out of the dungeon, but I was being taken to Foss's home, which held a different kind of fear for me. Foss hated me, and there was only Jamie to keep him in check now. My eyes glazed over as Jamie's horse followed Foss to my new wretched home.

Six.
Guldy

"Hold on, Lucy. Don't pass out on me," Jamie urged through gritted teeth. He could no doubt feel my grip on consciousness wavering. Every gallop brought a torturous jolt to my ribs, meaning his ribs were also feeling the brunt of the aftermath from Foss's rage.

Jamie shed his invisibility as we rounded the corner and crossed over into Foss's estate. Foss had a huge piece of property with dozens of slaves working in his field. The long ranch house sat half a soccer field's length from the barn and the shed.

Foss dismounted and stalked toward the house, shouting over his shoulder to his head servant. "Viggo, this is Prince Jamie from Tonttu and a new slave I acquired. See to it they're taken care of."

Viggo whistled, and two men came trotting out from the field. He helped Jamie dismount and untied my rope from the horse. Jamie tried to help me down, but he could not raise his left arm without his ribs pulling painfully.

"Come on, little one." Viggo reached for me, but I backed away from the foreign hands. He had slicked back hair that was tied in a ponytail and dark eyes that were vacillating between authoritative and gentle.

My eyes darted around for the best way of escape. Jamie was off the horse, so I knew I wouldn't get far before my head would keep me from leaving.

I shook my head at Jamie, eyes wide with the fright I would not voice. *No. No, Jamie. No.*

Viggo gave me a sad smile. "These are the friendliest hands you'll see, so best not resist them just yet. I'm not a born Fossegrimen, so I don't bear the curse. You've no need to fear me."

I kept my mouth shut through my muted scream as Viggo grabbed my hips and pulled me gently down. He sent the horses off with one of the men. Viggo bowed his head to Jamie, who was holding his ribs in the same way I was. "Prince Jamie, do you require a doctor?"

"Yes, we both do." Jamie gripped my elbow to hold me upright.

Every step was a stab, and every breath an effort. Viggo looked me over and then lifted the leash over my head. "You won't run, will you, Guldy? Can I take this off and trust you'll not make my life harder?"

I nodded, but refused to speak to him or anyone.

I walked behind Jamie and Viggo to Foss's house, my head pointed to the ground so no one would feel the need to smack me around. Just like when I was a new kid at school, I knew to keep my head down while I gauged the law of the land. If this was my new life, I'd survive until my own will gave out, not until Foss ordered my ending. *I* would decide it, not him.

Viggo whistled for a woman he introduced to me as Erika. "She's going to take you to get some women's clothes and get you cleaned up. She'll show you around Master Foss's property."

As long as I lived, I vowed I would never call him Master Foss. I would sooner have him break all my ribs than debase myself that low.

"What's your name?" Erika asked, her black braids swishing as she talked. She towered over me, but she still seemed youngish, perhaps my age. Erika spoke to me like I was a fragile bird, which was actually pretty well spotted.

I don't know why I would not answer her. She seemed nice enough to warrant at least a response. But I knew if I opened my mouth, I would start crying, and I would not break on Foss's property like that. He hated my weaknesses, so I would show him and his people none. I kept my head bowed and shook it slowly, hoping she would not be too pissed off at me.

Viggo motioned for Jamie to go down the hall as we entered the solid wood ranch that belonged to my third worst enemy behind Pesta and the Mouthpiece. There were red tapestries that stretched from ceiling to floor with gold cords wrapped around them. Fossegrim was hot, but the shade of Foss's home added a note of cool to the air, though I still could not relax as Erika led me through the main hallway, toward the side of the house, and back out another door.

Viggo spoke to Erika as a mix between an equal, a boyfriend and a boss. I was having a hard time getting a read on him. "She'll be Guldy until she feels like correcting us. Run along, Guldy. Erika's nothing to be afraid of."

Erika bit her thumb in his direction, like a jab, but with an edge of flirtation mixed in. "That's not true. I've been known to tan a few hides when certain people step out of line."

Viggo chuckled at her. "Then I'll be sure to jump clear off the line next time we're alone."

She shot me a look after he disappeared that said, "Men! Am I right?"

In another life, we might have gotten along swimmingly. But in this life, I would hold tight to my personality and give it to no one, since I could already feel it slipping through my fingers.

Erika led me to the bath house that was at the end of a path to the left of the actual house. There were three rooms, one for men, one for women and the third for Foss and his guests. She handed me some soap, a towel and a brown dress, but did not leave to give me any privacy as she filled the tub. "Hand over your clothes, Guldy. I'll wash them and give them to Master Foss. Maybe he'll be able to trade them for something useful. Maybe a young boy might want them." She eyed my jeans as if she very much doubted it. "How old are you? You're so much shorter than us, but your face looks like you're of age."

I didn't answer. Instead I shot her a sort of smile that showed her I understood, but was not ready to talk yet. Lucky for me, she was much like Tonya and didn't need a second person to have a full conversation.

"Because that's a child's size. Hope it fits. Might be a little short, but there's nothing like flashing a little ankle to catch a man's eye. Though Viggo's spoken for, just so you know."

I raised my eyebrow as I kicked my shoes and jeans off, wishing for a little privacy, but knowing I'd get none. I tried working off my shirt, but my ribs were too badly bruised to allow for much movement.

Erika helped extract me from my shirt and gasped. I covered myself as best I could, but there was no point.

"Nøkkendalig!" she exclaimed. Then her arms were around me in a hug so fierce, it nearly made me break my vow of silence just to get her off my sore ribs.

She realized her mistake and released me. "Does Master Foss know? I'll tell him straight away. The doctor's coming to look at Prince Jamie, so he can examine you while he's here." She helped me into the tub with great care, for which I was grateful. "So, what happened? How'd you escape? Who was your master before?"

Visions of Nik saving me in the water from the Nøkkendalig flooded my brain, only to be stamped out by images of his broken and bloody body on the shore after he destroyed his people's portal.

I shook my head at Erika. *Nope.* Wasn't ready to talk about it.

"What's Prince Jamie like?" she asked girlishly. She looked to be barely twenty. She had tanned skin and her long black braids hung around her head like tassels, swishing from side to side when she talked animatedly.

I shrugged in answer. What could you really say about Jamie? Nice guy. Prince. Lost his best friend and his sort of fiancée and was stuck with me for life. Lucky guy.

Erika took the soap and started washing my arm. The sweetness of the gesture endeared me to her. Then it dawned on me she probably thought I was mentally challenged or something. I probably looked like a wild animal. No speech, weird clothes, dirty as all get-out, and could barely move without wincing.

"You're lucky Master Foss bought you. You have no idea how bad some of the other masters are. We've got it great here. He feeds us well, doesn't take any of us against our will, and doesn't give us too much that we can't handle. You should hear some of Viggo's stories from his time with his old master. Trust me. You may not know it yet, but it's a good thing Master Foss found you."

I wanted to vomit, but my stomach was empty. Yeah, Foss was a real peach. Thank my lucky stars the man who hates me and pushes me around now owns the deed to my life.

Erika washed me until I took the soap from her and finished up. I dried off and stepped into the dress, which Erika helped fasten for me. The brown hem fell just below my knees. Erika's was to her toes. I'm guessing this was a big deal because Erika giggled at my pale shins. "It'll have to do. It's either this or something like my size, which would just fall right off you." Erika was the standard six and a half feet tall with a curvy figure like Marilyn Monroe.

Sure, I'll wear a child's dress. Why not? My life's pretty much maxed out as far as humiliation goes.

Erika led me around the grounds, and despite my aching ribs, I was able to walk mostly upright so long as I held onto my side. She introduced me to around seven dozen slaves, who greeted me with genuine and reassuring smiles I did not understand. They were enslaved, and yet they seemed fine with their lot in life.

"Viggo!" Erika called when we returned to the ranch. "Where's Guldy supposed to be working?"

Viggo came from Jamie's room and looked me over in my new digs, smiling at my shins as Erika had. "Master didn't say. She's too small and pale to be of use outside. Maybe in the kitchen? House slave? Keep her with you for now. Master's hosting guests tomorrow, so Brenda's going to need extra hands in the kitchen."

"Oo! Anyone important?"

"Only the chief, Master Olaf and Tomas of the Hills."

Olaf? Probably a pretty common name.

This was apparently good news, because Erika clapped her hands together like a schoolgirl and let out a high-pitched squeal.

I missed Tonya.

"There's always a big feast when the chief comes to visit. There's dancing and singing. You'll love it. Perfect welcome to your new home." Erika took me to the flour-dusted kitchen and introduced me to a bossy woman named Brenda.

Big-boobs Brenda was no one to be trifled with. While she accepted my muteness as a blessing, since I would not talk back to her, she did not love my inexperience with de-feathering a chicken.

I held tight to my vow of not crying on Foss's property, but there were a few touch and go moments. I was beginning to understand why my mother had always been a resolute vegetarian as I plucked each feather from the poor bird's skin.

Brenda's hand flew out and slapped me upside the back of my head. "You take too long! You're being stupid on purpose. Give me the chicken. Just what we need, another one like Kirstie. Pretty and useless." She yanked the bird from me and ripped out a quarter of the feathers in one go. She shoved it back onto the cutting board. "Now you do it."

I gulped and ripped, hating myself and silently apologizing to the chicken. Brenda picked up my hand and examined the size, shaking her head at my uselessness. "There are five more when you're done with that one. If you want to eat before nightfall, you'll have those in the oven before I finish with the bread."

Erika rolled her eyes behind Brenda's back. "Kirstie's the master's favorite. Of all the women, he takes her to his bed most often, and she never lets us forget it."

"Just because she's useful in the bedroom doesn't mean she should be allowed to neglect the other rooms." Brenda punched and kneaded the dough as if it offended her, her enormous breasts swaying with each whack. Her red face was sweaty, but her gusto was never compromised. I finished plucking the poor chickens too slow for her liking, but she didn't hit me again for it, so I guessed I hadn't failed too badly.

She handed me a cleaver with some level of expectation, but for all my youthful experience, I'd never deboned a chicken. Erika barked at Brenda when Brenda smacked me over the head again.

I was really beginning to like that girl.

Erika took the cleaver from me and hacked the bird down the middle, demonstrating what I was supposed to be doing.

"What do you want from her? She's obviously not right in the head, Brenda. She just escaped the Nøkkendalig."

Brenda and two other women nearby gasped. "The Nøkkendalig?" Brenda looked at me with new light. I was not useless. I'd somehow escaped the men that drove fear into the hearts of all women. "How did you get away?"

I swallowed my self-loathing, took the cleaver and slammed it down hard on the naked bird as Erika had done by way of an answer.

Brenda took a step back from the obviously unbalanced girl. "Are you Mare?"

I shook my head and finished deboning the chicken in front of me, and then moved on to the next. The women fired their questions at me, but I would not answer.

Seven.
Hulk, Smash!

The doctor came to examine Jamie's ribs, and Erika beckoned him to look at mine. She showed me to a room and made to leave me with the man, but I held onto her hand and shook my head. The physician looked nice enough, but for some odd reason, I didn't have any trust left for him.

Erika understood and sat on the bed with me, holding my hand and running her fingers over my arm as the doctor moved my dress so he could examine the wound.

"Huh. The exact same as the prince's," he mused. "Plus a run-in with the Nøkkendalig?" He gave me a nod of appreciation as he fingered my sore ribs. "Well, it looks like you won't be held back by a few bumps. Nothing's broken, so you'll be okay in a few days. Try not to use this side until you're feeling better." He looked inside my mouth and in my eyes. "See she gets some water. Some food. Whoever owned her before Master Foss didn't take very good care of her. I don't know what accounts for her stature other than malnutrition."

Erika nodded. "I'll tell Master Foss first thing."

Though he'd just seen my bare torso, he looked at my shins with pink cheeks as Erika buttoned me back up. "See she also gets some decent clothes. Master Olaf and his men are coming to visit tomorrow night, I hear. Best not be flaunting her in her damaged state."

"Of course," Erika agreed gravely. When the doctor left, she helped me off the bed. "The men here won't do anything you don't want, but Master Olaf isn't as strict about that sort of thing as Master Foss. With hair like yours, you're very fortunate Master Foss found you first."

If I made it out of this ordeal a virgin, I would thank my lucky stars. One day years from now, I would process all of this and freak out accordingly. For now survival was key, and to survive, I needed not to think too long on the horrors of the day.

I wanted to go into Jamie's room and hide, but there was work to be done. Whenever I checked in on him through our bond, he was in the throes of anxiety over Britta and Jens. I wasn't ready to feel that.

"It's your first day here, and the doctor said not to use your ribs too much," Erika argued when I followed her back into the kitchen. "Go rest. No one expects you to jump right in on your first day."

Brenda looked very much like she wished to argue this point, but out of respect for the handprints that were still scarring my body, she stayed her tongue. I made my opinion clear by picking up a dish in the sink and washing it out. Maybe I couldn't pluck a chicken, but I could definitely wash a dish. If I could be Queen Lucy, I could sure as smack be Slave Lucy with just as much dignity. *Suck it, Foss.*

"Is that her?" a feminine voice asked with unveiled disgust, hands on her generous hips.

"No, this is the roast duck Master Foss brought home. You can see it's a new girl." Erika's snotty tone almost made me smile. I did not look up from my task to greet the new person.

"I thought Viggo said Master Foss bought a *woman* for the house. She can't be older than twelve."

With an obvious lack of fanfare, Erika droned to me, "Guldy, this is Kirstie."

Kirstie moved to where I could see her if I looked up, but I was intent on keeping my eyes on the dishes. In my periphery, I could see she was curvy with thick lips and a pinched nose. Her black hair was partway pulled back, but some was left down to sway as she moved. She sized me up to see how much competition I presented. "I'm Master Foss's bedslave," she bragged. That was her tone, at least. Why she would brag about that was beyond me. "His *only* bedslave."

Message received. You've got the burnin' loins for Foss. I wanted to laugh in her face at the stupid thing she felt the need to stake her claim on, but I kept my head down. She lost interest after a few more minutes of prodding for information I would not give.

The house filled with the scents of freshly baked bread and roasted chicken as the day wore on. Erika showed me how to hand wash the clothes, how to beat out the rugs and how to change the linens throughout the house. She introduced me around and acted as my own personal mouthpiece, which was fortunate since I was bent on not speaking.

Dinner was a strange affair. There were two tables, one for the slaves and one for the real people. Foss sat at his table, and then motioned for Kirstie to join him. It was clearly a position of honor, and her bountiful hips swayed as she made her way to his side, kissing his cheek before taking her seat.

Jamie was holed up in his room still. I began to appreciate how great a guy he was that he didn't throw his royalty card around and make it seem like the mere act of eating with him was a privilege.

Though the tables were separate, the servants were not afraid to converse with their master. In fact, they were not afraid of him at all, but held an admiring respect for him. He was served his meal first and asked to tell stories of his journey to Tonttu.

Foss was certainly less surly than he'd been on the trip. He kept the details of the mission to himself, instead spinning it as a personal invitation to dine with Prince Jamie, and in return show the prince the Isle of Fossegrim.

I stared at my plate as he spoke, clanking my silverware so it appeared I was eating. The water could not be resisted, though. I tried to remain firm in my no eating or drinking policy, but my mouth was the Sahara, so I downed my water and felt it splash around my hollow stomach.

Everyone was glad to have their head of the household home, but I wanted out. I wanted a real bed. I wanted normal things and a life where I could look men in the eye without getting backhanded. I wanted out of this stupid mission. There was a part of me that resented Uncle Rick for putting me in this position, knowing that my own father never would have put me in such danger over and over again. I began to understand that Uncle Rick loved me only as much as he was capable of it, which was, well, not enough. I was a tool to be used for his greater purpose. Although I now shared his goal, I resented him for putting me in harm's way. For not loving me more than his mission. No wonder Mace always looked so lonely.

A few of the servants tried to draw me into conversation. I nodded along when appropriate, but said nothing. Throughout the course of the meal, they began to accept that I was mute, shifting prods for conversation to simple yes and no questions.

The men at the table didn't feel as dangerous as Foss or the evil smackholes who frequented the slave trade, but their eyes on me were not indifferent, either. I shrank as much as I could and kept my head down so as not to encourage any advances I could tell were on the horizon.

I felt eyes on me, but it was not the familiar feeling of Jens. I kept my head down and fiddled with my fork some more, ignoring the heat coming from Foss's direction. I wanted to flip him the bird and snap at him for staring, but I maintained my stoic silence.

When dinner was over, I set to work in the kitchen doing the dishes. Brenda closed down the kitchen alongside me, and I could tell she was grateful that I helped without being asked or told what to do.

Everyone else was bathing and getting ready for bed when Erika came to fetch me. "I put your mat next to mine. If Viggo comes to sleep next to me in the night, don't be afraid." Erika led me toward the back door, but Foss called out from his room to her.

"Erika, bring me the new one. She'll share my bed tonight."

My skin crawled with such disgust, it was a wonder I didn't ralph all over the wood floor.

"Yes, Master Foss!" Erika turned to me with junior high-like excitement on her face that I'd been chosen for a prom date by the hot senior (which, incidentally, had never happened to me). "It's a big honor, Guldy. Master Foss usually only takes Kirstie into his bed. Oh, that'll teach her to lord her position over us!" Erika hugged me, ignoring my stiffness.

I shook my head vehemently, motioning that I wanted to go with her.

Erika frowned. "But you can't turn down the master. No one turns him down."

Images that terrified me to my very soul were conjured up of me in Foss's bedroom. I wanted nothing to do with him or that room. I continued to shake my head. When she looked even more confused by my opinion, I walked in the opposite direction of Foss toward the shed where the servants slept. He'd bought me as a slave, and I'd sleep with the slaves. Let him explain that to my uncle.

Viggo and Erika ran out to me just as I reached the shed. "Wait, Guldy. Did you not understand?" Poor Viggo still thought I was slow in the head. "Master Foss has chosen you to warm his bed tonight."

Aw, barf. Now there's that image in my brain. I shook my head and pointed to the shed, walking inside to find an empty mat among the servants. I laid down with my back to the wall so I could make sure no one came at me from behind.

Viggo scratched his head and made his way over to me while Erika twisted her hands in excitement. Viggo knelt by my head and spoke softly. "If the master requires you, you must go."

I clung to my mat as if my life depended on it, shaking my head adamantly.

"Are you a maiden?" he asked delicately.

I buried my face in my mat to escape him and that question. I liked the fact that I was virgin, don't get me wrong. I just didn't enjoy my business being the topic of conversation.

Erika shook her head. "She can't be. She's been attacked by the Nøkkendalig."

"Ah." Viggo nodded in understanding. "It won't be like that."

Just then, the door to the shed burst open, and I half expected Foss to shout, "Hulk, smash!" Instead he bellowed, "Lucy, I told you to come here!"

When I only clung to my mat harder, he stomped through the shed, parting his servants like the Red Sea. They scattered out of his way, clearly confused at seeing their master so angry, and a slave so rebellious. He snatched me up and carried me out of the shed over his shoulder.

Oh, I wanted to beat on him. I wanted to pound my fists into his back or his kidneys or spine or whatever would hurt the most that I could reach. I knew if I did strike him, his retaliating blow would be far worse. He carried me past Kirstie, who was red and fuming that she had been dethroned by someone who clearly did not want the post.

Foss dumped me on the floor of his bedroom from his staggering height of seven feet. When I slammed down, my ribs jarred anew. I let out a single cry before stapling my lips together. I scrambled on my hands and knees toward the door, but he slammed it shut. "Stop it, Lucy. You'll stay in here tonight."

I clutched my knees to my chest, crossed an arm over my breasts and shook my head. The romantic fireplace. The let's-get-it-on bed with crimson sheets that took up a third of the room. Panic rose in me as I clutched the hem of my dress and tugged it downward.

Foss held up his hands with a look of disgust. "No, no. I won't touch you, I promise. When Alrik catches up to us, I don't want him to find out I made you sleep with the slaves. My men probably wouldn't try anything, but you'll be safer in here."

His words were confusing me. It was almost like he was trying to be nice, but was so befuddled with the emotion that he had to throw me on the floor first.

"Get in the bed," he ordered.

I smacked my hand to the wood floor, staking my claim that the hard surface would be a fine enough bed for me. If he didn't like it, he shouldn't have pushed me down.

"Don't be difficult. I've had a long day too, you know. Do you think I want to fight with you about this?"

I crawled over to the furthest corner from his massive straw bed and curled up in a ball on the floor.

He sat on the bed, took off his shirt and ran his

hand over his face. "Look, I know you're mad at me for hitting you after I bought you. But I'm a big name in my country. It won't do for word to get around that common slaves feel free to look me in the eye. My own people can, but not random slaves. What I did sent a message to the other girls there. People watch what you do, Lucy. I can't have them emulating you on my conscience. They start looking their masters in the eye, and they'll get far worse than sore ribs."

When I said nothing to this and did not even acknowledge he spoke, he threw his arms out and started yelling. "What do you want from me? Jamie already chewed me out for it. He says he's too sore to get out of bed. How are you already doing chores?"

Because I'm not a wuss, I wanted to say, but in reality I knew that Jamie preferred his privacy for his grieving. He had given up hope that Jens was still alive. Waiting for Britta was torture for him, not knowing if she would be caught and imprisoned by the Nøkken for aiding Nik.

"You don't have to do chores anymore. You're my bedslave now, so your job is seeing to my needs." He shook his head as he kicked off his boots. "Don't worry. I won't need you for that, but it'll keep you close and give you a reason to stay off your feet for a while until you feel better."

He paused and watched me stare lifelessly ahead. What was he expecting? For me to thank him? *Thank you, Foss for making me your fake whore. I'm so lucky to have a big man like you to smack me around.*

"Fine! Sleep on the floor for all I care." Foss stoked the fire before flopping down on his bed. I could tell he'd missed his home. The comfort it brought him and the familiar feel of his own bed relaxed him more than I'd ever seen.

It was too much. Unbidden tears welled in my eyes, and I cursed myself for drinking the water that made those abominations possible. I laid down and shoved my hand to my mouth to keep any offending weakness silent while I wished for anything to feel familiar ever again.

Eight.
Fighting with Foss

Foss had locked Jamie in his room during the night to keep a cap on the siren's curse. I had awoken a few times to the sound of the prince pounding on his door, rambling incoherently like a madman. Instead of going to Jamie, I gently coaxed him into my imagination. I conjured up a soft bed for him to lay on and wrapped him in the thickest feather-stuffed blankets I could think of. I made him imaginary hot cocoa and lay next to him, stroking his curly brown hair until he calmed down.

At one point in the night, Imaginary Britta knocked on the door to our fake room. When she came inside, Jamie leapt up off the bed and attacked her with passionate kisses that made her yelp in surprise.

Then she pushed him away, choking on something I couldn't see.

I noticed a red stain on her chest. It began to grow, spreading out and covering her whole upper body in drippy red that made her fall to the ground as she choked, dying at Jamie's feet.

Jamie was beside himself, losing his mind trying to save her to no avail.

Without a word, I removed his hands from her dead body and pushed my dead BFF back out into the hallway, shutting the world out and locking us inside.

I love it, and it dies. I love it, and it dies. Over and over, Jamie chanted the horrible phrase I admit I'd thought on more than one occasion.

No, no. That's not true. It's all a dream, Jamie. It'll pass. Jamie's subconscious wept with such woe that I took him into my arms on that pretend bed and rocked him, kissing his forehead. *It's okay,* I whispered to his temples. *We don't know anything for sure. Maybe they're all fine. Maybe they're just taking their time coming over because they're sick of Foss.*

All Jamie could do was chant Britta's name over and over in a mournful manner. My heart felt the pull for her, as well.

"Stop it, stop it!" I heard Foss shout, breaking me out of my dream state. Jamie and his bedroom vanished from my mind as I opened my eyes.

I was surprised to find Foss wasn't in bed anymore, though it was still the middle of the night. He was kneeling on the floor next to me with a look of grave concern laced with fear on his face. His hand was on my back, and I realized I was sitting up, clutching my knees and rocking. I released my grip on my knees and let them drop to the ground like limp noodles, leaning back on Foss's arm.

"You were sleeping sitting up and rocking like a lunatic! That can't be normal."

I squinched my eyes shut and tapped my forehead, and then pointed in the direction of Jamie's room.

"Jamie? Is he alright? I locked him in his room so he wouldn't attack my household." He postured, but then relaxed when I nonverbally assured him that Jamie was alright; he was just having a bad dream.

Foss shuddered. "A terrible curse, your mind wandering when you're supposed to be asleep." His hand rubbed slowly up and down on my back, and for a few minutes, I forgot to hate him. "Strange that your people dream all the time."

I nodded. I enjoyed my dream life, but Jamie's was awful. I don't know how he managed it all before he had my subconscious to escape into.

Foss brought me an extra pillow from his bed, laid me down and covered me with a blanket, knowing I did not want to lie in his bed with him. It was sweet, so I immediately suspected he was up to something.

I had a hard time falling back to sleep after that.

I awoke the next morning to the sound of the servants bustling around the house. Foss was getting dressed, so I kept my eyes shut and hoped one day my brain would reset itself so I didn't have to know what his firm backside looked like.

When I was sure he was fully clothed, I opened my eyes and pushed myself off the ground. My neck cracked horribly, and as I stretched, I knew I probably looked as bad as I felt. I hadn't eaten in days. I was sore from head to toe and had cried myself to sleep on the hard floor.

Whatever. Jens was probably dead. My family was dead. It was only fitting I looked like the zombie I was inside.

Erika tapped lightly on the door just a couple minutes later, introducing a tray of fruit and cheese to the room. She shot me a secretive smile before her face fell at my appearance. Yep. That sealed it. I looked so much like crap that no one would want to rape me ever again. Mission accomplished.

"Take her measurements," Foss ordered. "Have Axelia tailor a red gown to fit her."

Erika's mouth fell open. "A red dress? For tonight?"

"Today, if possible. Help her if she needs it. Lucy is the lady of the house. Quicker word spreads about that, the better, so don't hold back."

Erika bowed her head in my direction. "Welcome to the house, Lady Lucy." She took out a piece of yarn from her apron and used it to measure me as quick as she could with her long, nimble fingers.

I can't imagine I looked like I should be bowed to, so I stared up at Foss for an explanation once she left.

"Come here, rat."

Great. Back to that, are we? I obeyed to protect further damage to my ribs and walked over to where he sat on the bed.

"Still keeping your mouth shut? Good. That'll save me from having to shut it for you. Eat some breakfast before you go out there. You look terrible."

Pfft. Like it mattered how I looked. Don't need a beauty salon to wash dishes and cook all day. I turned on my heel and moved toward the door.

"I said it's time for you to eat! You've had your little fit. You made your point. I won't knock you around now that you're not out in public. Play by the rules and you'll be fine."

My hand was on the knob when Foss barked at me. "I said sit down and eat, rat!" He picked up a grape and ate it. "Is my imported food not good enough for you? Do you know how expensive this is? It's imported all the way from Tonttu! Do you know how lucky you are that I was the one who bought you? That you didn't get taken by someone else?

Fair point. The other guy had groped me. Foss had only bruised me pretty good. Oh, happy day. I should buy a lottery ticket with all this luck.

I made to leave, but Foss slammed his fist on the door, his form swallowing mine. "You'll eat and you'll be grateful," he demanded.

Oh, I wanted to punch him good and hard. I took a deep breath and tugged at the door, fruitlessly communicating that I wanted to leave his room.

Foss growled at me and led me toward the tray of food by way of a stiff grip to my upper arm. "If you starve yourself on my watch, Alrik'll have my hide. Don't be difficult. Jamie's wasting away no matter how much of my food he eats."

Oh, yeah. Forgot about that.

He picked up a piece of cheese, pried open my mouth and shoved it inside. I struggled in his stern grip to no avail. He clamped my mouth shut and pinched my nose, cutting off my air so I would be forced to swallow.

Two could play at this game. I stared him down as I ran out of oxygen, not worried in the least. He was only speeding up my inevitable demise. Save me the trouble of writing a suicide note to no one.

My crappy body took over seconds before I ran out of air and swallowed the bite I tried so hard to avoid. I pushed him away with a scowl that matched his and ran for the door.

"That's how we're going to play this? Fine!" Foss threw me down on the bed and pinned me there, shoving grapes in my mouth and cutting off my breath until I swallowed.

I ate seventeen grapes and five mouthfuls of cheese before he let me up. Still, he would not allow me to leave. "Now that that's over, I know you can pay attention. Jens was fine with you not fighting, but you're a liability to me out there if you can't even throw a decent punch."

I raised an eyebrow at him, not understanding what he wanted from me.

"Give me your fist." When I did not comply, he snatched at my arm and balled up my fingers into a fist. "Thumb on the outside, aim and punch. Try it." He held out his hands for me to aim at and nodded for me to attack.

As enticing as that was, I stepped back.

"Hit me, rat!" he bellowed. "Jens is most likely dead. Your uncle isn't here. No one's going to coddle you. It's time you learned to fight. I can't be watching you all the time, and I need to know that you and Jamie are solid backup."

His words stung me, but that never bothered him. I backed away further still, eyeing his hands warily. If only I could get to the door, I might be able to run away and get some distance from him.

"Listen, I'm having the other four powers over tonight to talk business and see if we can get some help getting closer to the portal. Some of their servants aren't as controlled as mine. I can't be thinking about the portal and worrying that you can't handle yourself without me."

When I shot him a withering look, he puffed out his chest and shouted, though I can't imagine why he thought shouting was necessary. I'd been mute for days. "Do you understand what I'm saying to you? Does your tiny brain grasp the situation? Blondes don't exist here, so you need to stay near me. If we get separated, you have to know how to defend yourself. Put up your hands and hit me!"

I looked down at my ineffectual fists and then turned my pitiful gaze up to Foss. It was hopeless. I'd never be able to fend off a gang of men his size.

Foss understood and softened as much as he was capable. "I won't tell you it'll be okay, because I don't know how this'll measure out. My men know to watch out for the women when we have guests, but I won't take chances with you. Alrik's got too much magic, especially now that Mace is off his leash. They'd make my life miserable if you lost your maidenhood on my watch. Plus, you know, the whole human portal that you have to destroy."

I hated that he pretended to care, and when he did, it was for all the wrong reasons. Nevertheless, if this is what I had to do to get out of here, I would do it. I put up my dukes and swung at Foss's hand, barely jabbing his superior reach.

Foss grinned, relieved that I wasn't completely

hopeless. "That's it. Now punch me like you're trying to escape the Nøkkendalig."

I shook my head, biting back a sob I would not let loose in his presence. What a low blow. I didn't want to think about that horrifying day. I could barely process the day I was currently living.

Foss pushed me further. "Punch me because you're angry Jens is dead! No one's coming for you!"

Leave it to Foss to bring out the worst in me. I swung at him, smacking my fist to his palm. I struck out again, missing this time, but the intent was clear. I gave up trying to hit his hands and aimed for his stomach, which was a far easier target to hit. I wailed on him, not caring if he was hurt or if he was instructing me how to better knock him on his backside. I punched him over and over, eventually checking him with my body.

That was a mistake. I guess the doctor wasn't lying about taking it easy. My ribs jerked excruciatingly, and I let out a bleat that was so pathetic, I was instantly ashamed.

Foss helped me to the bed and laid me down. I was in so much pain that for once, I did not put up a fight. I curled up in a ball on the mattress and sobbed. I was stuck in this horrible place with no way to get back to a normal so sucky, I had no real reason to return to it other than creature comforts.

I looked up at him and pointed to the spot my necklace had been, begging him with all I had left of me for him to find it and bring my treasure back. Bring Linus back.

"What? Your chest hurts?"

Yes, my heart is broken. I tapped my sternum and motioned to my neck.

"You have to talk if you want to be heard." Foss sat next to me on the bed, leaning against the ornately carved headboard as he stared ahead at nothing in particular. After a few minutes of respectful silence in which he gave me the space to have a breakdown, his voice settled on me in a quiet manner I did not often hear him use. "My mother was a slave for a very hard master. He did what he wanted with his property and didn't ask permission. I was conceived from her being taken against her will by him."

I stilled, quieting my crying to silent tears streaking down my face and onto the red sheet. He ran his hands over his jaw, clearly uncomfortable at having to share this bit of personal information. But as he continued, I could tell a load was being lifted from him. I wondered if anyone else knew.

"I grew up and became the best mercenary in the land. When I wanted out of that, I learned the fish trade, got lucky and built up my home. I went up to my old master's property and killed him in his sleep as a tribute to her. No woman has ever been taken to my bed against her will, nor that of my menservants." He exhaled out his demons and picked up a lock of my hair, twisting it through his fingers and examining the way the sun streaking through the window caught on the strands.

My hair was not for him to touch or admire. I sat up, turned around and socked him in the face, snapping his head to the side. The venomous hate felt good in my soul as it ate up the last of my vulnerability.

Foss was wrong about most things in life, but he was right about me needing to fight.

It was the moment of truth. Foss stiffened at the assault, inhaling slowly like a dragon readying its fiery breath. I didn't move. I couldn't breathe, for fear of his swift retaliation.

Foss swung his legs off his bed and stood. "Know your place," he sneered. "I kept you alive for Jens's sake, but I would caution you not to use up all my mercy. I'm not known for having much of it."

Nine.
United in Our Discontent

I was holed up in Foss's room. It had been a confusing day, and I only managed to get into more trouble the longer I was around everyone.

I'd gone out that morning to bathe, but Erika would not let me into the women's room. Instead I had to share a bathroom with Foss, like some leper from the female colony. My brown dress was absconded with while I washed myself and replaced with a well-fitted red gown that thankfully covered up my scandalous ankles, but coincidentally left my cleavage pushed up for the world to see. Aside from looking like a renaissance pajama dress, it was actually kind of pretty.

Erika had helped me into my gown as if I was so fragile, I'd forgotten the basic mechanics of clothing. Though, I really had no clue how to lace up the back, so she actually was very helpful. When I went to put up my hair, Erika insisted I wear it down on Master Foss's orders.

If I was speaking to him, oh the earful he would be subjected to. Ribbons and flowers were braided into the tresses, and if I wasn't so miserable, I would have been pleased at the whimsy of it all. If this was a Renaissance fair, I would've been like, Queen Wench of the Maypole or something.

When I tried to go about the chores for the day, Brenda shooed me out of the kitchen so fast and with such fear in her eyes, I wondered if Foss had sprayed bed bugs or something contagious on me. All the servants bowed their heads as I passed, but scurried away from me when I tried to make myself useful.

I went outside and tried to help the servants gather wood for the bonfire that would happen later in the night, but no sooner had I picked up a piece of wood did three servants rush to take it from me, rendering me useless.

Kirstie was the only woman with the guts to stare me down as I walked through the field. She had been crying, as evidenced by the red circles under her eyes. She glared at me as she bowed. At least her hatred made sense. I'd spent the night with her psychotic boyfriend. I'd hate me, too.

I gave her an apologetic half-smile, and she screamed at me, lunging for my hair. "You'll never be enough for Master Foss! His bed was mine to warm! He loves me!"

Oh, girlfriend. You done gone crazy.

Crazy, indeed. Kirstie knocked me down and ripped out a fistful of my hair, shaking it in my face as she cursed me to the never-loving place we don't mention in good company.

Viggo, blessed Viggo, was on her from out of nowhere. His arms wrapped around Kirstie and he backed her away, her heels skidding in the dirt. He got in her red face and shushed her while she screamed at me.

Erika ran to me and helped me up, brushing off my dress in fear. I ran back into the house. She followed after me, but I shut myself in Foss's room, shrieking when I walked in on him changing. He did not have the grace to look abashed or say anything to excuse his partial nudity. He took his time shifting his clothes into place, chuckling at my hand covering my eyes and my head turned away from the sight. "Boy, you are a maiden."

Maiden or not, I don't need to see his hairy mess.

Erika knocked lightly on the door, three polite raps to let me know she was there. "Guldy? I mean, Mistress Lucy? Are you well? Kirstie didn't mean anything by it. She's just upset, you understand. Viggo will see to punishing her. She won't try anything like that again."

Foss harrumphed and stomped over to me, looking me over to assess the damage. He glared at me as if I was the problem. "What did you do now? I got you a nice dress, gave you back some status, and you're still causing trouble? I can't leave you alone for a second! You're the death of every man you know. Jens is lucky to be rid of you."

If I was a bull, I would be snorting steam. His verbal slap deserved a physical one. Now that I'd given myself permission to punch him, a hard shove didn't seem like such a crime. I postured, pressed my hands to his chest and delivered a stiff shove, glorying in the effort that proved I'd stood up for myself.

The victory was short-lived. When Foss mirrored my assault with a shove of his own, it knocked me on my backside in one fell swoop. I cried out on instinct. As my butt hit the ground, Erika burst into the room and threw herself on me, using her body as a shield between Foss and me.

"Get out, rat!"

I scurried to my feet and backed Erika against the wall, not willing to let her take any hits meant for me. I stared down Foss, who snarled at me. Two bulls locked in an eternal cage.

Erika wrapped her arms across my torso and squeezed. "Master Foss, no!" she cried, the shock of his outburst clearly scaring her. Apparently his temper flare-ups weren't quite so common when I was not in the picture.

Maybe it was seeing the betrayal in Erika's eyes, or maybe it was my constant state of dishevel that snapped sense back into him. Dollars to donuts, it was when it dawned on him how small I was in comparison with the two of them, and that I was standing in front of her to shield her from his wrath. Whatever it was, I was grateful for it.

Foss's temper calmed, and the tension in the room began to dissipate. Erika's grip on me relaxed, and my arms lowered from their shielding position. "I... Erika, what happened with Kirstie?"

With tears in her eyes, Erika whimpered, "N-Nothing Viggo isn't taking care of, Master Foss. She just got a little jealous that you've made Mistress Lucy your mate. She let her temper get the better of her."

Say what? I crinkled my nose in distaste as the significance of the red dress dawned on me. Why no one let me help with chores, and they all treated me like I was someone to be feared and respected.

"She ripped out some of my mistress's hair and attacked her. Viggo's handling it, sir." Erika hugged me from behind. "Mistress Lucy didn't do a thing to provoke her. You know how Kirstie feels about you. She thought you would make her your wife someday."

Foss deflated, shaking his head in disappointment at the drama. "Very well. You may go, Erika." When Erika did not move, Foss rolled his eyes and displayed his hands to her. "Your mistress is safe."

I nodded to Erika's questioning look, giving her what I hoped was a reassuring smile.

When she left, Foss sat on the edge of his bed and growled his frustration into his hands. "So it's clear to you and there's no doubt in your mind, you're ruining every bit of my life. I don't know how you manage to step on everything I have and then get me to feel sorry for you, but you've done it again. I meant what I said about Jens being better off dead than with you. You wear calamity like a wreath around your neck, and now it's fallen to me to keep you alive for the rest of the journey. Your presence is a curse to me, and if I die in this, I'm certain the fault will rest on your bony shoulders."

If he expected a response, I did not give him one. My mouth was sealed shut, lest I open it and let him know he'd hit an organ I needed to survive.

"That being said..." Foss took the gold ruby ring off his finger and examined the cuts in the stone. He jerked me forward by my arm and closed my fingers over the heavy piece of jewelry. I gave the hammer and squiggly swirly design on the gold a look before I handed it back, but he shook his head. "It's my signet ring. Not exactly how I imagined this moment. Not with Kirstie, either, but you're the absolute last person I would want to be my wife."

My head shot up and my mouth fell open in shock. I shook my head, horrified that this was his proposal. I was appalled that he was proposing at all, really, but the double layer was that it was in the cruelest way possible. Forever I would remember the first man who proposed to me. These were my memories now. This was my life.

I wanted no part of it.

I shoved the ring back at him, mustering up the most hurt expression I could throw at him without tearing up and stomped toward the door.

Foss was on his feet, but he was not as angry this time. He was defeated as he held the door shut to stay my escape. He drew a leather lace from his pocket and slipped the end through the ring. "Lift up your hair," he instructed, this time without so much aggression in his words as he stood between me and the door. I obeyed, my doom sealed as he tied the leather string around my neck, marking me as his for the world to see.

I was not his. I belonged to Linus. To my parents. To Jens. To me. I didn't want his necklace where Linus should've been.

When his arms retracted from my neck, I burst into tears, clawing at the leather and wishing for it all to just go away. For him to go away. For me to be gone.

In a move so unexpected, it set loose more tears, Foss drew me into a hug, covering me with his massive arms. He sank down the length of the door to the floor, taking me with him. Because I had no one else, I cried into his neck, pounding my fist to his chest when the anger at the deterioration of my life grew to be too much. He let me beat on him in my pathetic state until I exhausted myself. I slumped in his arms and finally just let him hold me.

A sort of peace settled in around us, unexpected in its beauty, but most welcome, given our usual state of unrest. His hand rubbed my back to comfort me, and I pressed my ear to his firm chest, confirming that yes, in fact there was a heart beating somewhere in the depths of him. This was not the life he wanted, either. We were united in our discontent, and for now that would have to be enough.

He was agile as he stood, sweeping me up with him without too much jostling. Foss carried me to his bed and covered me with his sheet, doing the things I guessed he rehearsed in his head that he would do if he ever had a wife.

In the quiet of the moment we reached a fragile truce of sorts. It was not forgiveness, but it was a start.

He sat on the bed and leaned forward, resting his elbows on his knees, head down as he spoke to me in a quiet, even voice. "Tonight matters a lot to the mission. If I can't get close to the portal, I won't get out of this ordeal alive. You may not care about my life, but my household depends on me. I cannot let them down."

I lay on my back and blinked up at him, letting him know I understood the stakes.

"You're my... my wife now, so you have to obey me in public. If they see you disrespecting me, it'll break down the chain of respect I need to keep a firm hold on my estate."

I nodded slowly and tried to be a team player. If this was what was required of me, I would do it. I sat up in the bed facing him and drew my knees to my chest.

Foss explained the way of the world, talking with his hand perpendicular to the bed for emphasis. "You'll eat at my table, and when I say eat, I don't mean push the food around on your plate. You'll smile at my guests and be nice no matter what you think of them because you're the lady of the house, and it's your job to make the men feel welcome. You'll learn how to oversee the servants in time." He eyed me. "You'll speak."

I was onboard until that last note. I shook my head to tell him that just was not possible right now. When my family died, I didn't talk for a whole month, maybe more. I lost track of the days that piled up before Tonya coaxed a few words out of me.

Foss nodded. "In time. Maybe Jamie will come out of hibernation by then. He's better with your female emotions than I am."

Understatement, buddy. Whenever I checked in through the bond with Jamie, he was either sleeping or mourning Britta and Jens. As much as I was hurting, I couldn't put anything more atop Jamie's shoulders. I worked on thickening the mental wall between us, knowing he couldn't take much more sadness seeping through from my side.

I held up my fist, but Foss did not understand the

gesture. I molded his fingers in the same fashion and bumped his to mine, nodding that the motion sealed the deal.

"Oh. Okay. Is that from your world? We don't do that here." He spit into his palm and extended it to me. I crinkled my nose in disgust, but eventually did the same, cringing when our wet palms touched. I wiped my hand off on his pants, making him laugh. "I guess it is strange. But look at you, learning your part. When we get to your land, I'll make sure to play along with what's expected of me."

I smiled and mimed my evil plotting face, feathering my fingertips together like a true villain.

I don't know how we managed it, but Foss and I got through the next few minutes without fighting. We talked and mimed amicably until Erika came to fetch us for lunch.

Ten.
Lady of the House

Lunch was strange. I ate at a table much too tall for me not to feel like a child at. Brenda's homemade bread and stew made my stomach scream and nearly jump out of my body to get at the food. For once I answered the call of my hunger's incessant clawing. As I ate, I noticed Foss relax.

The lively chatter that had happened the night before was muted as the servants watched us eat. Kirstie was still red-faced and filled with visible loathing toward me, but she did not fly across the room and rip out more of my hair, so I guess that was a plus.

I grew self-conscious with seven dozen people watching me eat my roll, so I put it back on the plate and stared at my hands, wondering if I'd done something wrong already.

"Is no one hungry today? Perhaps I should tell Viggo you've not been working hard enough." Foss looked up at his head servant, gratified when they stopped staring at me and dug into their meal. "Will things be ready for my guests tonight?"

"Yes, sir. We're ahead of schedule in case Master

Olaf comes early, as he did last time."

Foss and Viggo conversed about the party while Kirstie practically burned a hole through me with her heated stare.

When the conversation fell to silence again, Viggo stood and held up his cup. "I see you've decided to make Guldy your wife, Master. Many happy years to you both." He raised his cup in a toast to us, which many of the others mimicked.

Kirstie did not salute us. *Good for you, girl. I'd be pissed, too.*

Foss raised his hand to acknowledge the toast. He looked at me, and I could feel how utterly disappointed he was with his lot in life. I bore his discontent with shame, but reached out and held his hand to show his household we were a united front. It was my greatest acting feat to date.

I watched Foss's spirits lift a little. He sat up straighter in his chair, now that he knew I wasn't going to be difficult. He placed a kiss to the back of my hand and thanked Viggo for welcoming his new... wife.

I hated my life, but at least I wasn't in danger of getting backhanded anytime soon, since I was holding the hand that would swing out at me if I took a step too far out of line.

My first official task, after I ate enough lunch at Foss's table for him to be satisfied, was to bring Jamie his new clothes and coax him out of his room for the party. Foss walked with me to the long hallway and pointed to the room at the end. "That's the prince down there." I bumped my fist to Foss's and watched him smile. "Thank you. I know you hate this, but thank you for not making it all harder than it has to be."

I bumped the crown of my head to his chest, closing my eyes for a moment so I could pretend he was someone I sought comfort from.

He sifted his hand through my curls, taking pleasure in the one aspect of me that did not irritate him. "We won't be here forever."

We parted ways and I went to Jamie's room with Erika, who was now my constant shadow. After an unanswered knock, I opened the door to find the prince on his bed, staring up at the ceiling. The interruption from his seclusion drew his eyes, but he said nothing by way of a greeting.

I put my hand on his forehead and then lifted his shirt to examine his ribs. His body was fine, but as I had been, he was buried in depression. He'd known Jens a lot longer, and he'd only just come out of his shell of proper behavior around Britta. Now they were lost to us. I understood.

I excused Erika from the room and latched the door shut behind her. His food tray was untouched on the wood floor, so I picked it up and brought it to his bedside. When he did not sit up, I hovered over him and covered his chest in a hug so I could lift him up. When he was finally sitting upright, I settled in between his back and the headboard, rubbing his shoulders in solidarity. He leaned back against me and sighed, his eyes welling up at my touch that brought him comfort he did not want to feel.

I kissed his temple and hugged him, running my fingers through his curly brown hair as I had done in the dream we shared in the night. I leaned him up against the headboard and pulled his tray onto the bed. Lifting the bowl, I spooned a bit of the stew into his mouth.

"He's gone," Jamie whispered mournfully. "He's gone, and Britta might be in a Nøkken jail right now. I denounced my family for her. We were engaged. I offered to take it back, due to the disrespectful way I asked her, but she refused. She wanted me, even though I'm laplanded. Even though I'm no one's first choice. Even though I'm third-born. Even though I'm cursed. The most beautiful woman in the world wanted me."

My heart swelled and burst like a water balloon for Jamie's plight. I fed him a few more bites before he realized he was being spoon-fed and took the bowl from me. "Thanks. Any word from the others? What's Foss heard?"

I shook my head, handing him his roll. I patted his pile of clothes, indicating he should wash up and change. He finished his meal in his haze and stood, taking his clothes out into the hallway.

Seconds later, he burst back into the room. "You're wearing a red dress!" he accused. His eyes fell to the ring on my neck. "Lucy! Jens's body is barely cold! How could you marry another man? It can't be Foss. You hate each other!"

I stood and closed the door behind him so his voice did not carry to the servants. I touched the ring and shook my head, letting him know I wasn't really married.

"Why aren't you talking?" He touched his throat. "Wait. I can talk, but you can't?" He looked me over, taking in my sallow complexion. "Oh, you won't." He watched me tap the spot where my Linus ashes used to be, and I explained the significance to him without words. "Oh, Lucy. I'm sorry, *liten syster*. I understand. But why did Foss dress you up like the lady of the house? That's his signet ring, you know."

As if on cue, Foss let himself into Jamie's room, his voice low as he spoke. "Could you keep your questions quieter? I don't want the whole household knowing our marriage is a sham."

"What?" Jamie whipped his head between Foss and me, begging for an explanation. "How long was I in here for?"

"Long enough." Foss postured, causing Jamie to stand straighter. "You've had your time to mourn. Now you stand like a man. I've got men from all four tribes coming to a feast here tonight. I'll try to persuade them to our side so I can get to the portal when it's time. The portal's been closed off since word spread of the Nøkken's being destroyed. Security's too tight for me to get through on my own, and then get out alive." He pointed to both of us. "So I need you two sharp for tonight. Jamie, you need to lay your royalty on thick so they feel the need to impress you. And Lucy, keep the drinks coming. If they're sloshed, they'll be more likely to agree to help us."

I nodded, glad that I had a role in the plan.

Jamie gestured to my dress. "Why is she wearing privileged clothing? Why's your ring around her neck?"

Foss grimaced. "I couldn't think of any other way to keep her safe. It was a bad idea. The powers are coming tonight with their servants. Some of their men aren't as well-behaved as mine, and I owe it to Jens to keep her maidenhood intact. He saved my life with the cave trolls." He rubbed the back of his neck, hating having his gratitude known. "I was pinned down by one of them, and he killed it, taking a pretty bad blow so I could escape."

I cringed. I hated when he talked about my virginity.

"Okay. Alright." Jamie chewed on his thumbnail and looked me over. "Is there any way to hide her hair?"

I motioned cutting it off, and Foss, of all people, protested the idea immediately. "No. My servants saw it first thing when we got here. There was no point in hiding it. Word's already spread to Olaf's camp that I have a Guldy on my property. It's one of the reasons he's agreed to come."

My nose crinkled in disgust. I didn't want to be paraded around, but as I looked down at my dress and touched the braids and ribbons in my hair, I realized that's exactly what Foss was doing. I was the prize pig, and he was bragging to all the locals that he'd bagged a blonde. Men are gross.

Foss stared me down, unwilling to let our truce break so quickly. "Play your part, Lucy. This is how you can be useful to the team, so do your job. Smile at my guests and keep the Gar coming. Pretend you're madly in love with me, and we'll get out of here with no one the wiser." He eyed his ring on me with an unfathomable expression. "Don't worry. That ring won't be around your neck forever."

Eleven.
Olaf's Plan B

I stood next to Jamie with the worst fake smile plastered on my face as a cavalcade of black horses arrived. Viggo and his men stabled the beasts in the freshly cleaned stalls as Foss greeted his guest of honor with a kiss to both cheeks. I was thrust toward the man, unable to attempt invisibility with so many eyes on me. The chief's men eyed me appreciatively, but also with a note of confusion. Foss had gone into town to run an errand an hour ago, but I was glad he'd returned before his guests arrived. I didn't feel confident enough to hold my own in this world.

"You've taken a child for your bride?" the chief questioned Foss. He had long trimmed sideburns stretching down the sides of his face to his closely-shaved beard. It was cut to frame his thick lips. I guessed him to be somewhere smack in the middle of his forties.

Foss postured. "She's twenty. Her height's the tradeoff for her hair."

Since apparently they'd not met any blondes before, they accepted this farce as truth. I was excused and all but ran to the kitchen, hiding myself in the mountains of dishes. I got halfway through the pots when Brenda and Erika came back from setting up the food outside on tables that had been brought out for the occasion.

Brenda gasped at my damp sleeves. "No, Mistress! I was just getting to those pots. Out with you!"

I turned to her and shook my head, my fear clearly displayed.

Erika understood. "You're hiding out?"

I nodded, grateful for her once again. I put my hands over my hair to show her I didn't want them to see me.

Brenda cottoned on to my concern. "Very well. You can stay, but you can't be seen doing housework. Master Foss would have my hide." She brought in a chair from the dining room and pointed to it. "Have a seat." Brenda took over where I left off with the dishes while Erika whisked cream in a bowl with some sugar. "Most of the master's parties are a grand affair, but Master Olaf's men are not of good quality. The women usually hide in here." She let out a belly laugh, her enormous breasts shaking like jelly. "Men have no idea what to do in a kitchen, so it's a safe place, indeed."

Erika laughed and I cracked a smile, glad that someone made a joke, and I understood it. I decided to hole up in the kitchen as long as I could.

That timeframe was longer than I had hoped for, but an hour later when Kirstie came to fetch me for Foss, I still was not ready. Brenda noticed my trepidation and tapped me under my chin so I would stop focusing on the floor. "Now, now. They can smell the fear on you, so best not show them any. Go out, do as Master says, and when they're all smashed, scamper on back to me. It'll all be alright."

I threw decorum to the wind and wrapped my arms around Brenda, wishing my own mother was here to tell me everything would be fine.

Brenda stiffened, and then chortled softly, patting my hair with unconcealed affection. "Run along, Guldy."

I smiled at the use of the nickname. I followed behind Kirstie, who grew frustrated at my lack of understanding of their culture. "You have to walk in front of me," she ordered as we moved outside, the warm air doing nothing to relax my nerves. "Don't you know anything? You're the entertainment. Foss wants to show you off to the men." With an evil laugh, she whispered in my ear, "Olaf's got hands like leather and breath like death. Enjoy his eyes on you all night long." She grabbed my arm and pushed me forward toward the lion's den.

The important men were sitting at a grand wooden table on a raised platform in between the house and the vineyard, while nearly three hundred servants all sat on the grass at a lowered table about knee-high. When I approached, Jamie stood, his gentlemanly manners foreign to this area. Foss raised his ornately carved cup to me and kicked the chair next to him out. What a sweet invitation.

My heart froze along with the rest of my body when I saw one of the guests was none other than

Gropey McGroperson, the man who considered buying me from my cage while sizing up my breasts. Bald head, scar down his right cheek, sweaty face, beady eyes and breath like the worst mixture of sewer and landfill were only a few of the things that made me cringe. I took my seat and kept my head down through Foss's welcome toast to his guests, clutching Jamie's hand under the table. Olaf made no indication we'd met before, though I could tell he remembered.

The second Foss finished his grand greeting, Erika, Brenda, Kirstie and seven other women brought out the food on platters, serving us first, and then the servants below. The warm evening air crackled with the nearby bonfire as we ate root vegetables and beef. It was delicious. Though to be fair, my stomach was pretty starved, so it accepted with gratitude whatever I fed it. I shoveled food in my mouth as I did my best to hide behind Foss's girth to shield me from Olaf's view.

There was lively chatter, and the three other guests of honor asked me several questions that thankfully all had yes or no answers.

Tomas of the Hills had only a passing interest in me, for which I was grateful. His wife was also dressed in red. She'd smacked two servants across the face before she finished with her main course, so I decided we probably wouldn't be besties anytime soon.

Olaf belched loudly like a true Viking barbarian. He had a woman on his lap whose body he was very free with. She did not wear a red dress, so I guessed she was his Kirstie equivalent. "What a lucky man you are, Foss. To find her in the trade? I wish I'd known she was such a prize."

Foss grunted in response. He glanced over at me and noticed my extreme discomfort. His arm wrapped around my back drew me closer to whisper something in my ear. "This is me saying something to make you smile." He waited a few seconds for my mouth to comply. "Now I'm being charming." I pulled back and cast him a withering glance, which made him laugh in my face. It was rare he was genuinely entertained and let it show. He kissed my cheek, which is when I noticed he had beef juices on his chin that were now dampening my face. *Sick.* I picked up my cloth napkin and dabbed at his chin.

He grabbed my wrist, freezing us both at the odd shift in our dynamic. The look he gave me stayed my disgust at his lack of basic table manners. It was confusion and a small dose of wonder mixed in that we silently communicated to each other. We shared a small half-smile, just enough of one to mingle together and make one whole positive expression. I threw caution to the wind, kissed my index finger and pressed it to his lips for the benefit of his guests. The hardness in his black eyes softened, and he drew my stool yet closer to his so I was pressed to his side.

Foss was many things, most of them inappropriate to say in good company. But that night, we pretended to care about each other, allowing a mutual appreciation to begin to bloom. I put on my best adoring wife eyes, and he was kinder to me. His shoulders relaxed, and eventually I sunk into his side, trying to appear as if I had not a care in the world, thanks to my chieftain hubby. I finished the meal with his arm around me. To everyone at the feast, we passed ourselves off as a newlywed couple.

The other three chiefs had either wives in red dresses or mistresses who sat next to them or on their laps as the men drank. I was happy to sink into the background, swallowed up in Foss's side, but he was in the full swing of the moment. He pulled my stool between his legs and leaned me backward so my back rested against his solid chest that was much bigger than necessary.

Two servants whose names escaped me began playing fiddles around the fire, then three more, and more after that until dozens of fiddles were singing and lifting the spirits of everyone in attendance. All the servants either clapped, snapped their fingers to the tune, or twirled around the fire under the dark night sky. They were alive with the freedom that came with music, and that evening, lusty delight belonged to slave and the owner alike.

I caught Brenda's eye and motioned for her to get the head table another round of Gar.

There was so much merriment, Foss forgot himself and kissed the back of my hand as we watched a few of the chief's slaves put on a little dance show for us. He rested my fingers on his cheek and sighed contentedly when I began to stroke his jaw. He tickled the sensitive inside of my arm, relaxing me despite my surroundings. I wanted to question every move, but I was too comfortable. As dangerous as Foss was, I knew that he was the least of my problems. In this strange world, Foss was my safe place. It was a sad thought, but I did not stray from his side the entire dinner. He talked with the other chiefs, discussing commerce and the changing tides while lazily twirling a lock of my long hair around his thick finger. I knew Olaf was watching us, leering as if through a window. Wanting to steal, but unable to touch. I never thought I'd be super grateful for Foss, but that night I was.

"Now, Olaf. You can see the girl's spoken for," the chief reprimanded with a tease in his tone when Olaf made his third crude joke about my body.

"Yes, *Dom*," Olaf replied, turning his focus back to his Gar.

The chief was actually not too bad a guy. He seemed to be the most revered of the four powers, so when he asked me to dance, I guessed accurately that refusing him wasn't an option.

The chief was the standard Fossegrimen seven feet tall, wide-chested and tanned skin. I didn't know the first thing about how to dance with someone his size. I wasn't an excellent dancer to begin with, unless you count doing the Running Man, which didn't seem appropriate to this joyful jig.

I recalled one of Uncle Rick's childhood lessons about the Fossegrim. They could persuade people with their fiddle music. I was grateful the merriment that was being suggested around me was not coercing me to behave like the women who started dancing on the tables. I guessed since I leaned more toward my human genetics than Undran, their magic didn't work on me, just like Nik's hadn't.

Nik. The second the hurt surfaced, I stuffed it back down. I glanced up to the head table and saw Jamie touching his chest, my pain slashing him by accident.

I cast up an apologetic look to the chief for the

terrible dancing that he was about to endure from my end. He held my hand and tipped his head in an impression of a gentleman. He seemed to understand and danced more slowly with me than the others swinging wildly around us.

The chief was powerful, indeed. He did not dance to the music, but the music slowed for him. The merry ditty melted into a soft sway.

"I never thought I'd see the day Foss would let a woman into his home and give her his signet ring. You must know how lucky you are."

I nodded, offering up a pleasant smile to conceal my grimace. He held my hand in our slow sway, and I could see small bits of silver glitter on his fingers and wrist. It was so uniquely decorative for the man who otherwise appeared a Viking; I didn't know what to make of it.

"I'm the power of the North, so officially I don't have any favorites, but unofficially, I have a special eye for Foss and his affairs." The shine in his eye mutated to a hint of a threat. "That you slipped onto his property without my knowledge is a great surprise to us all. I didn't know Foss was looking for a wife. I had many I could have offered him, forming an even stronger alliance between the North and the East. What did you do to capture him so suddenly?"

I managed not to get killed off yet, I thought bitterly. To answer him, I showed him my hand and made a fist, and then punched the fist to my chest, holding it there so he could see Foss and I were joined by something strong enough that an offer from a competing woman would not be considered.

The chief mulled over my answer as we swayed. His trimmed sideburns were long, stretching to the bottom of his jaw, and moved with his face when he talked. "Foss is not a born power. He worked hard and fought his way up the ranks to become what he is now." His look down at me suggested a warning. "It would be a shame if anything were to compromise that. A shame I wouldn't hesitate to rectify by removing the problem and dumping it in the ocean."

I gulped and nodded, turning my face up to him so he could see that I wasn't plotting anything evil against Foss. They had a sweet relationship, a sort of father-son thing. I didn't want to do anything to wreck that.

"That's a good girl."

I could feel Foss staring at me, so I caught his eye and offered up an encouraging smile, letting him know all was well. He nodded, shoulders relaxing as he returned to his conversation with Tomas of the Hills.

It was a small movement, so discreet I might not have caught it if I hadn't been looking in that direction right then. The generous-breasted woman on Olaf's lap leaned forward in a gusty laugh and sprinkled something into Foss's drink.

I gasped, stiffening in the chief's grip, and tried to end our dance.

"You're finished with me already, Guldy? Well, that's a first. I've never had a woman try to leave me alone when there was music about."

Afraid I might be beheaded for something stupid without warning, I communicated the fear I felt with a look of pleading for him to follow me to the table.

The chief indulged me, only because he probably

thought I was unbalanced and didn't want to offend Foss by letting his crazy wife wander off.

I pushed my way through the dancers and fiddlers to the head table, snatching the goblet from Foss just as he was reaching for it.

Poison! Olaf's girl poisoned Foss's drink, Jamie! Say something!

Foss's stern expression that I'd publicly embarrassed him by taking away his Gar like a child shifted to fury when Jamie pointed his finger at the woman on Olaf's lap. "Lucy saw Gerda poison your drink, Foss! Don't touch it."

Olaf did a great show of being outraged at me, a woman taking a drink from one of the four powers. I trembled as he motioned for two of his men to come and take me away so the party could continue.

I clung to the chief, fear muting the force of my determination that Foss should not drink from his cup. The chief held up his hand, and the fiddling stopped. The servants all fell to their knees where they stood in deference to their leader of leaders.

"Your bedslave has been accused of poisoning the great power of the East. What say you, Olaf?"

Sweat was pouring off the bald man, but he managed to keep his cool, sneering to cover over the fear I knew was there at getting caught. "I say the Guldy's seeing things. She doesn't speak. She clearly doesn't understand our rules. Gerda was just refilling his cup. Being a good host while the Guldy was keeping you entertained." There was a claw of malice and jealousy of Foss's favoritism from the chief hidden behind every word. I knew Olaf was a danger to me, but seeing that he was a threat to Foss steeled my resolve.

I gently tugged on the chief's sleeve, bringing him down to my level so I could lean up on my toes and whisper in his ear. "I saw her put something in Foss's cup. I don't know what it is, but I'm guessing that's not something you would let someone do to you." I placed my other quaking hand on the chief's bicep, and I could feel his body leaning in toward mine. "If all she did was refill his cup, then make her drink it in front of you. I don't care about your rules. I won't let Foss get hurt." Then I pulled back and looked deep into the chief's black eyes, seeing a person buried beneath the curse. I pressed my fist to my chest again, reminding him that Foss and I had a strong bond. "If you love Foss like I do, you should protect him."

The challenge in my tone could not be ignored. The chief answered my hard look with one of his own, and then postured. "What a fine idea. Gerda, finish Foss's Gar."

Gerda looked positively ashen. "W-what? I'm sure I couldn't disrespect one of the four powers by drinking from his cup. I'm not worthy."

Nicely played. I stood straighter and met Foss's thunderstruck gaze. I nodded, letting him know I was on the mark.

Foss stood, handing his cup to Gerda and wrapping her fingers around it. Loud enough for everyone to hear, he said, "If my wife saw you poison my cup, then you will drink your medicine." He addressed the sweaty Olaf, who vacillated between sick and fuming. "Olaf, you will control your woman. This is my house, and this is what I wish. If she did nothing,

I'll take my wife out back and flog her myself for her insolence."

I paled as I gripped the chief's strong arm, hoping he might save me from this nightmare.

Olaf appealed to the chief. "*Dom*! This is madness! Surely you don't believe Gerda would do such a thing."

The chief placed his hand atop mine, assuring me that he knew I was spot on. "You'll respect Master Foss, Gerda. Drink the cup if he orders it so. You're on his property, so you'll obey one of the four powers."

Olaf buried his face in his bedslave's shoulder. "Drink it," he commanded.

"Master!" she cried, tears spilling down her cheeks at the betrayal. It was no doubt his idea that she'd carried out. I felt for the girl, but before I could come up with a plan that wouldn't kill her, Foss and Olaf were pouring the drink down her throat.

"My bedslave would never poison you," Olaf challenged. "She respects the four powers and wouldn't think to..."

It was a thing of fortune the poison was fast-acting. It was as if Olaf knew his time to distance himself from the act was nigh and tumbled out as many words as possible to excuse himself from the crime and pose as an innocent bystander.

Gerda choked as foam came up from her stomach and pushed out of her mouth, burning her lips as it fizzled and popped down her chin. She collapsed on the table between Foss and Olaf, twitching a few seconds before her body went limp.

In that moment before the chaos broke around me, the thundering reality banged in my brain that her death was on my head. It was my plan to oust the poisoner. I had killed this woman who had never said a word to me.

Foss roared at Olaf, and the two shouted back and forth with such ferocity, I was terrified to be anywhere near the rage. Foss picked up a chair and cracked it over the dead woman for no reason other than to further piss off Olaf.

Olaf touched the hilt of his sword, and my heart froze over, pushing me into action. Foss was armed with only his rage, which, granted, was a decently powerful weapon.

Olaf's men touched the hilts of their swords in unison with their master, and I saw in that moment the well-constructed plan of the sweaty man.

Plan A: Olaf's bedslave poisons Foss. Olaf wins.

Plan B: Olaf's bedslave is caught in the action. Olaf waits for Foss to Hulk out, and then stabs him in the chaos.

The great villains always have a plan B.

I forsook the chief and ran to Foss, jumping up and sliding over the table in my dress. I leapt onto the nearest chair and pressed my hand to Foss's chest, begging him with my eyes not to strike me as I balanced on the chair.

I spoke loud enough so my words carried to the people, my voice scratchy from disuse. "Darling husband, you almost died! You're so wise that you saw through her lies."

I stared into his black rage, communicating that throwing a tantrum in front of his guests would only start a war. It was important Olaf's clan remain the evil ones in everyone's eyes. It was vital the dead woman be seen as a sign to the others not to try something like that again, not because they feared him throwing a fit, but because he didn't need chaos to kill. He could do it with a simple command. "They're armed," I whispered through my adoring smile as I ran my fingers over his short hair, partly for show and partly to calm him down.

Foss didn't totally catch all my reasoning for stopping his tirade, but since I'd just saved his life, he sliced me enough of the benefit of the doubt. He played his part and wrapped his muscular arms around my waist, lifting me up an inch off the chair so he could show the people we were a united front. "You saved my life, lovely wife." The cheese was a little thick, but a few of the women swooned, so I guessed it was working.

Foss's fury melted, and somehow the crowd watching us fell to the wayside. "You saved my life," he repeated, but this time not for show. His gratitude was just for me. "You saved my life."

I shrugged off his thanks as if to say, "Yeah, I rock."

He smiled through his confusion as to why I would do something like that for him. "Lucy, you saved my life."

Then he did something I was not expecting. Foss pulled me closer, and I could feel his internal debate concerning his next move. He swallowed, searching my face for signs of something permanent, something he could latch onto.

I gasped when I felt his lips against mine, lighting me on fire with his very public kiss. Explosions and booms went off inside my body, confusing my worldview and knocking things off my neatly compartmentalized shelves. He scattered nonsense onto the floor of my fractured psyche. The heart that was mine and Jens's vibrated with the wrongness of the thrill that rippled down my spine.

Foss inhaled in surprise as his lips sought safe haven against mine. He deepened the kiss, gripping me tighter as he did so. The things we felt would never be spoken aloud, but they were there. Oh, yes. They were there.

Later I would rationalize my kissing Foss back by saying it was for show. But when I slid out of Foss's arms onto the raised platform for the elite, I yelled at myself inside my head for the true reason.

Confusion.

There should have been no confusion, just a swift kick to the groin to be delivered later when the show was over.

For a flicker of a moment, I was confused, and that transgression seared my heart as Jens's dead body floating in the water plastered itself in my brain.

Foss shook his head like a horse, attempting to right the wrong.

Jamie took a shot of Gar to clear away the sour taste in his mouth from my sudden attraction to Foss. I could tell the ripples of my physical and emotional swell echoed through to him.

Everyone was applauding and hollering at our explosive kiss, but I wanted to run as far away from it as I could. I wanted to run to Jens, who was most likely not there to run to anymore.

"String up the body, Viggo," Foss ordered. He cast

a hard look at Olaf, who was red with his two failed plans. "You gave up your rights to bury her when she attacked me on my soil. She'll be strung up as an example of what happens when you cross one of the four powers." His chin rose, and I could see why people followed him. "Do you disagree?"

Olaf cast a pleading look to the chief, who was calm throughout the entire ordeal. "String her up, Foss," the chief ruled. "Let it be known that no attack on one of the four powers will go unpunished."

Viggo and a few of Foss's men dragged the woman off the table, and Olaf whistled for his party to pack up and hit the road.

The chief raised two fingers in the air and waved them around in a circle. "Liven up the night, boys!"

Fiddlers responded, eager to move on from what could've been a massacre. A lively ditty played while I turned my head away from the woman I'd killed as she was dragged off, my hand over my mouth to stifle any noise of distress.

Twelve.

Ally

It's okay, Lucy. You did the right thing, Jamie told me, catching my eye to give the terrified voices in my head reason to flee. *She almost killed Foss.*

I nodded, gulping as I tried to fade into the background. Foss pulled out my stool for me and lowered me down. I didn't notice I was trembling until he held tight to my hand and rubbed my back, leaning my head to his thigh. He stood around with the chief, Tomas of the Hills and Jamie, discussing the penalties for such things while I tried not to fall to pieces.

The chief noticed Foss's fingers winding themselves through my hair. The powerful man sat down on my other side, motioning for Foss and the others to take their seats.

I guessed the fiddlers were doing their best to lighten the moods, because everyone was remarkably upbeat, despite the horror that had just occurred.

"I guess I don't have to worry about your new wife being able to run your household," the chief commented, downing a shot of Gar and slamming the glass on the table. "I admit, I was concerned she would not be a good right hand, but after seeing the way she ran to you when she saw you were in danger, I guess I can stop worrying you've been bewitched. Were it not our people putting the sirens out, I would've thought you one of them, Guldy."

I didn't know what to say to that. I simply nodded and kept my head down.

The chief took another shot of Gar. His reaction to the taste was that of drinking because it was there and not because it tasted particularly delicious. "Foss has never taken a wife. I recall you mentioning something about women making men weak."

"This one always keeps me guessing," Foss replied, raising his hand in acknowledgement to a servant who toasted him. Foss leaned back in his chair and pulled me closer to him, as if we kicked back and watched TV together while we snuggled all the time.

Just then, a young girl came to the table and kissed the chief's cheek. "Papa, you said you'd introduce me to the Guldy," she complained.

"I did," he grinned. "I was just waiting to see what she was made of first. Guldy, this is my daughter, Aren."

I managed a weak smile, and wondered how the poor preteen was handling the scene I could barely stomach.

"You have lovely hair," she commented, eyes wide. "Master Foss must brush it all day long."

That'd be the day.

I'm not sure why I did it. Perhaps I was a little tired

of people reducing my value to a flip of the genetic pool. I combed my fingers through my locks and yanked out a few strands. I twisted them up and placed them in her hand.

Boy, was that worth the reaction. Aren let her gasp fly out in audible astonishment, marveling at the strands that I always got irritated with for clogging up my bathroom drain.

"Papa, look! So pale. So pretty." She looked up at me with rock star worship in her eyes and squealed. "Thank you, Guldy! Thank you, Master Foss!" She bowed to Foss, who acknowledged her curtsy with a polite bob of his head as he waved her away. She ran to her gaggle of friends and showed them the treasure.

Foss whispered in my ear, "Thank you." Then he brushed his lips to mine again. The kiss was tender and sweet, as if we were a married couple who did things like that all the time.

He did it because the chief was watching. That had to be the reason. The reason for the involuntary swoon on my behalf? No idea.

Brenda brought out more Gar, and more, adding to the liveliness of the night. Jamie drank steadily through the meal, asking for more Gar as soon as he emptied his cup. Even now that dinner was over, he continued his debasement. A few of the women started dancing on the lower tables, much to the enjoyment of the men. My eyelids drooped as I rested against Foss. His heavy arm wrapped around my shoulders and palmed my stomach as I laid back against his chest. His body was hard and strong. It held none of the warmth Jens's body did, but in this grim place, it provided a small amount of comfort. His thumb dragged up and down across my navel as he conversed with the chief.

The chief was cool once you got past the terrifying Viking-esque aspect of him. He and Foss shot the breeze while I sat in between them like a little mute doll whose hair Foss loved to stroke. The chief watched us with contentment plain on his face. "It does me good to see you like this," he said to Foss. "I confess, I never thought the day would come I'd get to give you your wedding present."

Foss raised an eyebrow, but maintained his laid back position on the chair. "A wedding present? Surely a good bride is gift enough, *Dom.*"

Barf. The words were so insincere.

The chief traced the lip of his shot glass as he spoke. "What would you say to taking the Tillbaka district off my hands?"

Foss's hand in my hair stilled. His words came out of him slowly, as if pulled by a cautious string. "Off your hands? Tillbaka? Are you certain?"

The chief nodded, still focused on the shot glass. "I am. You've more than earned it. It's high time your territory expanded."

Kirstie brought a round of shots to the table, shooting me a murderous glare. I made for double sure not to touch my glass. Not that I would've anyway. I mean, it's straight vinegar. Gag.

Foss was flabbergasted. "Thank you! Yes, I can handle the extra responsibility. You won't be sorry to've put your faith in me."

"Oh, faith in you's an easy bet," the chief complimented Foss kindly. "You've always been like a... Well, anyways, congratulations on your new bride. When she gives you an heir, you'll take over the Sötlands for me." He toasted me, cracking a smile at my wide eyes. "And you, Guldy, you can ask me for whatever you wish. One favor from the chief, so think on it wisely."

I touched my heart to let him know his gift was appreciated. I tried to push out thoughts of pink ponies and a white picket fence. Now was the time for strategy.

"That's... I don't know what to say." Foss ran his hand over his face. "Thank you."

I pressed my gold sandal down atop his foot under the table before he promised the chief something he couldn't deliver.

"A son," he crooned softly. Foss palmed my stomach again, tracing my navel and just begging for a punch in the face. It started out as a game of chicken, but now it was shifting to something unspeakably dangerous.

"You've proved yourself worthy." The chief didn't drink his shot, but kept touching the glass as if he meant to.

I leaned up and spoke softly, just loud enough for the chief to overhear through the lively fiddle music. "Darling husband, surely you have a better bottle of Gar for the chief. You don't want him drinking the stuff the servants drink."

Foss narrowed one eye at me, but conceded. "Why um, yes. I think I do have a few bottles I was saving for a special occasion." He motioned to the nearest servant to grab him what he wished.

"A good wife, indeed." The chief was happy at

being tended to as the king he was, and even happier when a bottle of hundred-year aged Gar from the Darklands was poured out for him. After three shots, I knew I could talk to him without fear of beheading.

"Are you enjoying your night?" I asked him. Both men took notice when I spoke, since it happened so infrequently.

"I am," the chief replied. "You? How do you like Fossegrim?"

I disregarded his question and went straight for the gut. "I think I know what I want for my favor now."

His eyebrows raised in amusement. "Shall I ready my stock of gold?"

"Wait, what are the rules?" I asked the two men warily. "Like, what am I allowed to ask for?"

"Anything," they replied in unison. Foss's hand stilled on my stomach, and I could feel his nerves building.

"I won't get in trouble? I want your word as one of the four great powers I won't get in trouble if I ask you for something big."

The chief was serious now, and I could tell his alert was going up. "On my honor. Whatever you wish. Though I would caution you to think on this. Ask wisely. It's one favor for your lifetime, so I owe you nothing after this."

"You owe me nothing now," I corrected him. "A favor is a gift. I just don't want you to chop off my head and string up my body if I ask you for something you don't want to give me."

The chief nodded, his jaw tense. "Then ask wisely."

"Will you walk with me?" I asked, noting the

number of people dancing around the fire who could easily eavesdrop if they meandered close enough.

"Foss, your wife's beauty is beginning to fade," the chief warned, standing and offering his arm to me.

My hand shook as I took his arm, letting him lead me off the raised platform for the super cool people and down toward the vineyard.

"I confess, I can't imagine what this favor might cost me," he said as we walked. We were on a slow pace through two rows of orange trees, just far enough away to keep our conversation private, but not too far to divorce him from the enchanted fiddle music that only played in my favor.

I stopped, and making sure we were alone, I grabbed an orange off the tree and sat down on the ground, motioning for him to do the same in the space opposite me. "Take a seat. I gotta think for a second." The chief looked around, hoping for invisibility so no one would see him sitting on the grass like a commoner. I rolled the orange toward him, and then held my hands out so he knew to roll it back.

"Guldy, you can ask whatever you wish," he reminded me, confused as to why we were sitting on the grass in the orchard, rolling an orange back and forth like children. He had to have been at least mid-forties.

"My name's Lucy. I'm not from around here. I'm not from Undraland. I'm actually from the Other Side."

He held the orange for a moment, considering my appearance. "That explains a lot. Go on."

"Don't throw the orange at me. Be cool until I finish, or you'll lose your temper, and I don't want that."

He squinted at me, admiring my gall. "I can be patient."

I gulped. "Have you heard of Hilda the Powerful?" I watched the chief nod. "Well, I'm her daughter." Then I held up my hands before he could freak out. "But I'm not a practicing Huldra. I don't have any magic in me at all. I'm totally human, nothing more."

"I saw no tail on you," he confirmed through tight lips. He gripped the orange with his glitter-spattered fingers, but then relaxed with a wave of his hand. "Go on."

"Now, be cool," I cautioned him, treading lightly. "My mother stole Pesta's rake long before I was born. Pesta's been tracking my family and trying to take us out ever since. She killed my parents, but didn't get the rake." I could feel nerves churning in the form of vomit in my gut. It was a reckless game I was playing, but I didn't see another way. "I got the rake, and now Pesta's Mouthpiece is after me."

He snarled, his thick lips showing his disgust. "Pesta. Why we weren't allowed to kill her is beyond me. And then they give her a Mouthpiece?"

"I'm glad you feel that way. I won't ask you for protection. Foss and my uncle can handle that. Do you know Alrik? Well, he's got the rake."

"Then he needs protection," the chief ruled. "You needn't worry about the Mouthpiece on the Isle of Fossegrim. Our ports are closed to him. Using a Grimen as her vessel was a marked mistake. There's no forgiveness for that."

I caught the orange and tossed it back. "Thanks for

that, but that's not my wish." I took a breath. "Foss doesn't know I'm asking you for this, so don't be pissed at him."

"Pissed? I'm sure I won't be mad at Foss. Marrying the heir of Hilda the Powerful? Risky, but so far it seems like he made a wise decision. I've learned not to question Foss. He always delivers."

"Thanks." I caught the ball and weighed it in my hands. "I don't want money. I don't want protection." I took a deep breath. "I want the Fossegrimen portal to the Land of Be torn down. Foss can do it using my rake, but I want your word you'll help him and that there won't be any retaliation."

There was a bug that wafted between us. Sort of a firefly mixed with a butterfly. Gorgeous enough to arrest my attention in the midst of the tense moment. "That's an *eld fjäril*. Lights up when a fire's near."

I watched the bug respond to the nearby bonfire. "You're probably wishing you got me a toaster or something instead of an open-ended wish for a wedding gift."

"I'm a man of my word, Guldy. I've been looking for a way to get rid of Pesta since the beginning. If you have the rake, I can grant you your wish."

"My very own Santa Claus," I marveled. "Thanks, Chief."

"Olaf won't be happy."

My expression of accomplishment fell into disrepair. "Olaf put his hands on me, so I don't much care what makes him happy. If tearing down the portal ruins his life, so much the better."

The chief raised his eyebrow at my accusation. "He

had his way with a wife of one of the four powers? And yet he breathes. How has Foss not retaliated?"

"Foss doesn't know. I've seen enough violence. I don't want Foss to fight anymore. Plus, it happened a day or two before we got married, so I'm not sure it would matter to him."

The chief grumbled under his breath. "Well, as you wish it, it shall be done. Let me know when Alrik comes with your rake, and I'll escort Foss personally to the portal. He has my full support. Pesta's seen her last soul from us."

I tossed him the orange. "You're cooler than I expected. Some of the other rulers? Not so much. Thanks." I stood and offered my hand to the chief. "Let's get back before you miss out on the good Gar." He stood and tucked my hand in the crook of his elbow. We walked almost like old friends back to Foss, who was vacillating between angry and afraid.

I kissed Foss's forehead, reminding him to calm down. "The chief's going to help you tear down the portal," I told him in a quiet voice. "No big deal, so you can relax now."

Foss's hackles rose. "What?"

The chief explained our conversation quietly to Foss and Tomas of the Hills, and after the litany of questions from both of them, a grave but hopeful understanding was reached. The men drank like friends and chatted about territories and animal predators sneaking food off the land, all the while thinking about the change of fate their land would undergo in the near future.

Thirteen.
Foss's Fruit and Fiddle

Foss's hold on me started out for show, but over the course of the night mutated into something more tender and less possessive. I was inexperienced with men, and wasn't used to them stroking my cheek or kissing my palm at every turn. I blamed the butterflies on my youth and lack of proper socialization. It was the only way to explain the jelly-like feeling my spine had when Foss paused his conversation to lightly kiss my lips again.

When it dawned on me that Jamie was drinking us both into a stupor, I poked Foss's ribs, interrupting his conversation.

"Whatcha got for me, Guldy?" he asked. The Gar and the narrow escape from death lifted his spirits considerably.

I tapped Jamie's shot glass with a clumsy hand.

"More Gar? Of course. Drink up, wife."

I shook my head, trying to make him understand before the haze took me under. I pointed to Jamie, and then to my head. I mimed drinking the Gar, and finally Foss got it.

"Oh, shite. Poor idiot's too miserable to think clearly. I'll take care of it." Foss made to get up and talk to Jamie, who was dancing over by the bonfire, but I turned and clung to him. He looked into my unfocused eyes. "Oh, yeah. You're halfway to sloshed. I'll be right back for you."

I gripped Foss's shirt and shook my head like a crazy person, silently begging him not to leave me alone in this world where I didn't know all the rules.

"Okay, okay." Foss smoothed the hair back from my face and took in my fear. "To bed?"

I nodded gratefully.

Sizing up my inadvertent buzz, Foss grabbed me a soft roll as he escorted me off the platform and through the partiers, giving a cool smile to the men who made lewd remarks about our honeymoon time as we passed by. He walked with me through the vineyard, occasionally pointing out an odd fruit. One that he showed me looked sort of like a big grape, but was too brightly colored to be so. He was chattier than I'd ever seen him.

"Eat, eat," he insisted, picking a circular blue fruit off one of his trees. It was smaller than an orange, but had the shininess of an apple. "Soak up some of Jamie's Gar. Most of the food in Fossegrim comes from my land, you know. The other three focus on lavender powder exports, but I keep us in fruit like this." He fingered the blue fruit with pride. "Keeps my men from wasting the day high, and keeps them loyal, because I feed them well."

I'd already finished the roll and was starting to think a little more clearly. I took a bite of the small blue apple-orange and nearly lost my lunch. Face contorted to a grimace, I spat the mouthful on the grass. My mouth was filled with lemon rind and something that tasted like organic dish detergent. I was allergic to lemon balm, and desperately hoped there wasn't any of that in this fruit's genetics.

Foss laughed like a younger man with no worries whatsoever. Head tilted back with levity at my plight, he barked his amusement at the giant red moon. "You're not supposed to eat it like that! You have to peel it. Don't you know anything?"

He pulled another off the tree and ripped through the thin outer membrane like he was peeling a clementine. I was still spitting out the remnants of the nastiness when he offered me a bite the way I was meant to take it.

I'd never been much of a foodie. I mean, really I ate whatever my mom cooked. When I was on my own, I cooked whatever was on sale. All the pasta and chicken in the world couldn't compare to the taste explosion that flooded my mouth when I bit into the meaty fruit. It was the freshest orange I'd ever tasted mixed with the flavor of something so tropical and sunshiny, I couldn't group it with any similar flavor. It was unique unto itself, and I couldn't get enough.

Foss broke me off another segment, grinning as I rolled my eyes in delight at the succulent juices that swirled around in my mouth.

When I finished off half the blue fruit, he looked over his shoulder to confirm we were alone. Then instead of handing me another piece, he reached out and fed it to me, his thumb dragging on my lower lip.

My blush couldn't be helped. I mean, it was so weird that he was being sweet to me when he didn't have to. There weren't any witnesses around. In fact, there was no one at all to see Foss lean down and kiss my lower lip, sucking the juices off it as if *I* were the fruit.

My stomach lurched with roller coaster surprise. I'm pretty sure I gasped. If in ten years I looked back on that moment, I might erase that part of it from the retelling. We were eating fruit in the orchard. End of story. There was no kiss. There were no butterflies in my belly. I certainly did not kiss him back, nor did I lean into the affection.

Foss's eyes flew open as he realized what he was doing. He pulled back and shook his head like a dog. "Cursed fiddles. That wasn't me," he said by way of apology. "It's the fiddles. All the music's messing with my mind." He rattled his head from side to side again as if he was trying to dump pennies out of his ear. "It's our magic. Fossegrimens can suggest behavior through fiddle music." He jerked his thumb toward the merriment we'd just left. "That song's to make us think we were..." He stood straight, puffing out his chest as if he needed to intimidate me. "But we're not."

My lips tasted like fruit and Foss. I could feel the pink in my cheeks and wished for Jens. I decided not talking was the only thing I had going for me at the moment, so I stuck with it. Jamie was still drinking, and try as it might, the bread and fruit were only fending off the inevitable. I really didn't want to be drunk in a vineyard with Foss. He looked like I was one wrong move away from him leaving me to make my way back on my own.

There was a rustle in the trees not too far from where we were. My alert went up; I was so used to danger at this point in our journey.

Foss focused his intimidation on the movement just out of view, shifting me to stand behind him. "Show yourself," he commanded.

"Apologies, Master Foss," a man said, stumbling forward as he fastened his pants. I heard a woman giggling behind a tree and saw Foss's shoulders loosen. The servant eyed me with a grin as he bowed to Foss. "Enjoy the night with your Guldy, Master."

The two ran back to the bonfire, laughing the whole way at being caught. Foss grumbled under his breath and stomped forward, expecting me to keep up with his long strides in my slightly buzzed state.

I made it into his house, passed the red tapestries and into his bedroom.

Foss built a fire for me, though there was no danger of a real chill. Undraland was pretty warm. The temperature vacillated only as much as a Midwestern state in the spring. He brought me another roll from the kitchen, taking a giant bite from it before handing it to me. The fiddle music wafted gently in through the window, reminding me of the merriment, but also giving me just enough space from the volume to allow my body to feel restful.

"In the bed with you. I'll not have you sleeping on the floor when there are so many about."

Though his words were unfeeling, he was careful

with me for once. I said nothing as he laid me on the bed as if it mattered to him how gently I hit the sheets. Some part of me knew it was a trick of the fiddle music, but I took what comfort I could get, however coerced into being.

I rolled over onto my stomach and tried to kick down the blanket to crawl under it, but Foss surprised me by taking off my sandals. His large hands didn't stop at that kindness, but began rubbing my feet to relax me, stroking my ankles with a slow seduction that made an unladylike groan escape my lips. It had been so long since I'd been good to my feet. The look of questioning I shot him was met with avoidance, as if he was not willing to admit with words that he was being nice to me.

He swallowed as the logs popped in the fireplace, casting an orange glow on the walls in the night. "You were helpful tonight. The men like looking at you."

I grimaced and slowly pulled my feet from his grip. If that "compliment" was supposed to make me feel awesome, it far missed the mark. I rolled onto my side and hugged myself, wishing it brought warmth to my unfeeling body as images of Gerda flashed through my mind.

Foss drew my long hair out from under me and spread it out on his pillow, staring not with hatred at the strands. His fingers combed through the tangles, watching with wonder the sight of my hair on his pillow. He hovered over me, lending his body heat to mine, and kissed my temple. Fiddles, indeed.

"You saved my life," he said again, a look of earnest confusion clouding the usual hatred in his eyes.

"Why?"

I still wasn't sure on the answer to that myself.

Without calling on the millions of reasons why I hated him, I turned, reached up from my reclined position and wrapped my arms around his neck. It was meant to be a simple hug, but before I knew it he was lying on top of me. I froze for a moment, and then gave in to the tenderness.

He slid his hands beneath me, indulging in the hug neither of us anticipated, nor would admit we needed that night. Halfway between my shoulder and my neck, Foss pressed his lips to my skin, savoring the intimate contact that was on the furthest reach of what I was comfortable with. There was no one to pretend for here. We were alone, and he was exchanging valuable time he could have been yelling at me to send sweetness into my body.

It made no sense. He never did.

I ran my fingers over his short hair, and we shared the same strange, relaxed air for a few breaths, indulging in... well, just indulging.

Foss tilted my head to the side, pulled my hair back and nuzzled me behind my ear, planting a kiss there as he inhaled the scent of my curls. It made me feel strange. It made me feel excited in a way I felt guilty for. It made me feel... It made me feel, and that was enough to give me the shivers.

When Foss finally pulled away to sit up on the edge of the bed next to where I lay, I couldn't believe how hard my heart was pounding, or that I was oddly sad to lose that connection.

He pointed out the window to indicate the music.

"Many children'll be conceived tonight. These are tunes for desire." He shook his head to rid himself of the hypnosis. "I went into town today," he said, reaching into his pocket. "I had to search out a few vendors, but I found it. Now, this better not be some stupid trinket from your world. I went to a lot of trouble to find it. Spent more money than you deserve." Then pulled out the most beautiful thing my eyes could understand.

It was Linus. It was my braided rope necklace with the glass heart that was filled with my brother's ashes. I gasped and let out a horrible sob, not realizing I had that many tears on standby as Foss hooked the necklace into place.

Suddenly, I was a little more me again. I felt one fifth more right in my sea of wrong, which was a significant bump. My hand trembled as it touched the heart to make sure it was really there. It hung just above Foss's ring.

The look of gratitude was the most I could muster through my relief that felt like helium to my system. I tapped the heart and sobbed in a mournful whisper, "My brother!"

"Your brother? He gave that to you?" Foss tried to understand. That he went to great lengths to find my necklace when he didn't even know what it meant spoke volumes of the loyalty we were beginning to share.

I swiped at my cheek and sniffed as the words came tumbling out of me. "No. This necklace *is* my brother. My Linus. My twin brother died last year, and these are his ashes. It's all I have left of him. Some days it's all I have left of me." I wept into my hands, not caring that he was seeing me fall to pieces. The dam I'd built up for survival cracked and broke all over the bed as I balled with relief over something I thought I'd lost forever. "I know you can't understand this because you don't need anyone or anything, but I *need* my brother! I need him, and that slave trader guy took him from me!" I tapped my Linus heart, and then I tapped my heart. My voice quieted through the gulps and emotional hiccups. "What you did? Finding this? I won't forget it. Thank you. From the bottom of my heart. Thank you, Foss."

Foss tried to wave off my sincerity, but he could not look away from the completely different person he was watching implode on his bed. He cleared his throat, steeling himself to speak what was on his mind. "My mother. She was killed and thrown by the side of the road while our master was out. I don't know what she did to anger him so. Not that he needed a reason. But when the caravan returned, she wasn't with him." He turned his gaze to his hands that were resting on his knees. "I searched all night and the next day for her body. I finally found her," Foss paused, and I could tell he was staving off unbidden emotion. "I found pieces of her with carrion birds all over her, picking away at what was left. My mother." He tapped his heart in the same way I had. "My mother."

I took my chance and gently tugged on his arm. He was so distraught that he permitted me to lay him down on the bed, resting his head on his pillow. I sat halfway up leaning on my elbow, my arm looping under his neck to cradle his burdens. His body was heavy with grief, so I rubbed his chest to soothe the ache there. "Tell me about her."

Foss shrugged. "What's there to tell?" As if asking himself the question, he began answering it after a moment's pause. "She played the fiddle better than anyone I've ever heard. Could bewitch the strongest will with a few notes. Taught me well, but since she died I haven't been able to pick up a fiddle."

I could understand that. Since my mother died, I hadn't felt music in the same way, either. "Was your mother tall, like you?" I asked, not wanting him to turn mean after his bout of emotional nudity.

He let out a toneless snort. "No one's tall like me. I'm tall like my master who raped her. I look like him. I got none of the good things from my mother." His expression was hard to keep the hurt from defining him, as it had me.

"Was she a hard worker?" I asked in a soothing voice, my tears falling to the wayside in light of his pain. I tried to keep my words from slurring, but the Gar was powerful.

Foss nodded, his gaze hollow. "Never let me see how tired she was."

I brushed my fingernails through his short hair, running my knuckles down his cheek. "Did she keep you safe?"

Foss scoffed. "Even her best couldn't do that, but yes. She did all she could."

I drew a small cross on his chest. "Then she's with you. I see how hard you work. I see you watching your servants." I spoke just above a whisper. "I think she'd be proud to know which of her qualities you inherited."

Foss rubbed a hand down his face, refusing to look at me. "You are not a bad wife, Lucy."

"And you're not a bad man. Stop trying to convince me you are." I dragged my fingers down his arm and held his hand, marveling at the size of his fingers. "I don't like when you shove me."

Foss kept his eyes on the ceiling and nodded, not willing to speak and risk showing emotion he could not deny in the morning. There was music outside and hundreds of guests, but we were quiet as we sat together. My vision began to blur until I blinked it back into focus. I could feel the drunkenness taking me down another layer.

"I should like to have a piece of my mother to carry with me, as you do your brother. I thought revenge would make me feel better, but it didn't."

He pulled me down next to him, which was a good thing, because I was feeling too tipsy for a graceful migration to the pillow. I collapsed in his arms, loving the feel of the burly man molding himself around me. "Thank you," I muttered, reaching up to kiss his cheek. "You did a good thing, finding Linus for me. Thank you."

Foss inhaled the top of my head and played with a few strands of my hair. "I need to go back out there. I'll cut Jamie off and send him to bed."

"Okay." I closed my eyes and felt him shift next to me, rolling on his side so our stomachs were pressed together. My mouth opened in surprise when I felt his lips pucker on my closed eyelids. It was the softest kind of gentle, and I felt goose bumps break out on my arms. "Foss?"

"Mm-hmm?" he breathed, his mouth just an inch from mine.

"I think your fiddlers are scrambling your brains again," I warned. I was warning him, of course, but I was also taking that moment to caution myself. The things I was feeling weren't logical, or even fully formed emotions. There was want, and I knew that was a dangerous thing when I felt Foss's thumb stroke my hip.

Then Foss pressed his lips against mine, slow and melty, filled with all the things I would never understand about him. This kiss wasn't for show. It wasn't passion, either. His kiss was something he wasn't used to expressing. We both knew the right words would never come to him, but I felt it. Foss was grateful for me. I could feel the emotion in his kiss as he deepened the affection, caressing my face, neck and shoulder.

It was wrong. I knew it then, even through my drunken haze. But that was us – all wrong.

He didn't rush the kiss or get too handsy. He didn't want me like that, which was a good thing. He moved slowly, pausing every now and then to kiss my cheeks or forehead to show how much he appreciated me.

It was two whole minutes before reason entered my brain. Two inexcusable minutes I hoped to forget by morning. I pulled back from Foss, pressing one more simple kiss to his lips that were growing eager. "Okay, I think that's about all I can handle. You're going to kick yourself in the morning for this. Or I will. We can't do this. I'm buzzed, and you're under the influence of fiddle Jiu-jitsu. Jens. I love Jens, and you hate me. I'm not ready to believe he's dead yet," I whispered. "But thank you for my necklace, Foss. Truly."

"Thank Jamie, but not like that," he warned with a tease in his tone as he fought to recover himself. "He told me you were missing it and described it to me. I confess, I never paid much attention to your jewelry." He shook his head to bring himself out of the fiddle's seduction. "And don't worry about Jens. He's probably not dead. I've never known him to tolerate defeat."

I allowed him to kiss me once more, a small peck on the lips like old friends or people who have been married for decades do. "Thank you, Foss."

"Consider it a wedding present," he joked. "Now will you sleep? I have to go back out and try to figure everything out with the chief and Tomas of the Hills."

"Sure." I motioned between us with a heavy hand. "And this didn't happen. I'm drunk and you're drunk on fiddle music. We're not us, so it didn't happen, got it?"

Foss looked relieved. "Smartest thing you've ever said."

"Here's another gem. The chief's bored with your Gar. If you want him nice and relaxed for your conversation about the portal, you have to keep the good stuff coming."

Foss could not hide how impressed he was with my helpful tip. "Not a bad wife, indeed," he repeated. "I'll see to it. I have another bottle of hundred-year-old oak-matured Gar."

"Sounds appropriately disgusting." I laid down, my fist covering my Linus heart. Foss tucked the covers around my neck, and I almost forgave him for being such a tool most of the time.

"I'll be back with Jamie so he doesn't make a fool of himself. Thanks for not embarrassing me tonight." He touched his lips. "And thanks for... just thanks."

"Don't mention it. Ever." I gave him a weak fist bump before closing my eyes and drifting off to sleep.

***

I had the strangest dream. Scissors cutting paper. Foss shaking me and yelling something... I don't know. Something. Jamie was stumbling through Foss's room, and the dream cut out again just as he was blacking out.

Fourteen.
Kirstie's Parting Gift

I awoke to the smell of Jens. It was the familiar scent of sugar cookies that made my spirits swell and swoon. I'd missed the smell of him so much, my heart hurt. When I opened my eyes, he was not there. Jens was probably dead, and the world still turned. The cookie smell was most likely Brenda making cookies in the kitchen in the middle of the night. I closed my eyes and fell back asleep to fend off Undraland a little while longer.

When the door opened several hours later, I turned to see Foss coming in carrying a tray with tea, a crust of bread and a few pieces of the delicious blue fruit on it. He gave me a forced smile to answer my tired salute, slid the tray onto the table next to the bed and sat on the edge of the mattress, covering his face with his large hands. Something caught my attention, and I reached up to pull his palm away.

I pointed at his black eye and silently asked how he'd acquired the shiner. No doubt his charming personality had something to do with it.

"It's a long story."

I moved to sit up, but he pushed my shoulder back into the sheets.

"We have to talk. Actually, it's probably best you're not talking today, because you're not going to like all of it." He took a deep breath, and I waited for him to gather his thoughts. "Good stuff first? Yeah, how about the good stuff first." He rubbed his palms together as he spoke. I could tell he was nervous. "The chief, Tomas and I talked all night about the portal, and the plan's a go. You were right about breaking out the good Gar last night. Or maybe I didn't even need to. I can't believe just asking the chief actually worked. The chief's been looking for a way to stick it to Pesta; he just didn't think we'd go for something so radical. Plus, we needed the rake, which thanks to you, we have now."

My eyebrows rose. That was certainly a good thing. I rubbed the glass heart on my sternum, drawing comfort from having my brother in some way with me. Another portal would fall, and this time without so much bloodshed. Thoughts of Nik weighed heavy on my chest. As much as Foss and I had our differences, I didn't want him to end up like that.

"Tomas is onboard, provided anyone who wants to go to Be is allowed one last chance. Not ideal, but it's fine. Olaf was against tearing the portal down at all, but he got outvoted. He's not pleased, but the chief was pretty mad at him when the conversation started out, so he won't cause a problem. Did I say thanks for saving my life?"

I nodded, a hint of a smile touching my lips as I lay

on the pillow.

Despite the great news, Foss still wouldn't look at me, nor did he appear relieved. "Okay. Now for the other stuff." It was then I noticed small pellets of sweat forming on Foss's forehead. "I shouldn't have left you here alone when I went to go get Jamie. I should've been watching how much he was drinking. I should've done a lot of things different."

I gave him a shrug. We all should have done things different. No use being so upset about it.

"Viggo warned me, but I didn't pay attention. I was focused on the mission. I should have kept a better eye on Kirstie. Maybe explained things to her. I don't know. Women are impossible."

I sat up and wrapped my arms around Foss. He was so distraught. I didn't understand all of it, but it couldn't be that bad. My neck felt weird, but I tried to focus my foggy brain on Foss for the moment.

He stiffened, and then deflated in my embrace. "You should stop being nice to me. Your boyfriend's already mad as a bull." He indicated his black eye.

Boyfriend? I guessed he meant Jamie. I wished he wouldn't make jokes like that. Jamie and I had enough problems to work through without adding nonsense labels that didn't apply to us.

He cleared his throat. "And that kiss was just for show, you know. Not worth mentioning."

I nodded, shrugging as if to say, "no kidding." We did not speak of the other kisses that happened in private. They felt like a distant dream, but in the back of my mind I could tell they were real. Both our eyes locked in on the blue fruit on the tray he brought me, and we swallowed thickly in unison at the memory of the juices he'd sucked off my lips.

"So, we won't mention it," he confirmed, just as relieved as I was not to have to look further at the mess. He cleared his throat again, and I could tell he was nervous. "Viggo told me Kirstie wasn't submitting to you as the lady of the house, but I didn't want to deal with her."

When I pulled back, I noticed the letter H on his shirt written in charcoal. I rubbed it off as he took the tea and food off the shiny silver tray. My neck was itchy, but when I moved my hand to scratch it, my hair was not its usual maze to get through. Just the ends of my hair brushed against my fingers. My brows furrowed together as I gripped my hair, letting out a choked scream when I found almost a foot of my curls had been hacked away while I slept.

Foss flipped the tray so I could see my reflection in the shiny surface. In black charcoal, I had "whore" written across my face, with half the H smudged from hugging Foss, who still could not look at me.

"She snuck in here while I was corralling Jamie, who was behaving like a drunken fool. She cut off your hair and wrote that on your face."

I examined my reflection with shaking fingers. I'd never seen my face with "whore" on it before, but now I knew I'd never forget the sight. I'd never had short hair, either. I always wanted to know what I would look like with it, but my parents insisted I keep it long. Linus joked that if I cut it off, no one would be able to tell us apart.

What was left of my mane was choppy and hung

just past my chin, uneven and crazy looking. I looked completely mental. For the first time in who knows how long, I saw myself. Bags under my eyes, thinned out cheeks and dry skin with fear etched all over me. Everything about my appearance was unsettling, but the fear was disgusting. That wasn't me.

I needed a rag, water and scissors. I swung my legs off the bed, shorn strands of my hair flying in the air and fluttering to the floor.

"I'm sorry, Lucy. I'm so sorry. I wasn't in control of my household."

Though I was upset, Foss seemed more disturbed by my appearance than I was.

"I put her out. Gave Kirstie to Olaf as a peace offering between our tribes. She won't bother you anymore."

My mouth fell open, but I did not argue his decision. I guess I was lucky all she did was mutilate my hair. I stood before him, just a few inches taller even though he was sitting down. I placed my hand on his shoulder and waited until he met my eyes. I shrugged off the horror and offered him my best "whatcha gonna do" face.

"Don't be nice to me. Not after everything that's happened. Kirstie stole the only good thing about you. You're hideous now, and it's my fault."

I flicked his ear for calling me hideous and reducing my worth to my looks. Then I went out to the kitchen to retrieve what I needed to clean myself up, ignoring Foss's call to me that he was not done talking yet.

I touched my Linus heart, relieved my brother was

somewhat with me through the ordeal. I know it sounds dumb, but the necklace made it feel like part of Linus was still with me. It seemed everything would be a little easier to figure out now that I had him over my heart again.

Erika was crying, actually crying about my hair and my face. That put things into perspective for me. I was getting upset over a bad haircut. There were worse things to cry about, so I saved my tears for a worse day. In Undraland, I was sure there'd be plenty to choose from.

Brenda ordered me to sit down so ferociously, I didn't dare disobey. She wiped off my face with a wet rag while Erika fetched me a new red dress that was less fancy, but still a notch above the brown house gowns the servants wore. She poured me some water and watched me drain the cup before letting me up.

Erika accompanied me to the bath house, insisting on scrubbing me down. She was in a more delicate state than I was about the whole thing, her tears mingling with the water from the sponge she dripped down my back. *Such drama.* Sweet girl, but the whole thing was a little melodramatic for me.

I took the shears I'd pocketed from the kitchen and went to work on what was left of my hair. Erika fetched the silver tray for me so I could see my reflection. It could have been a lot worse. My curls fell two inches below my chin, and I worked to add in layers so it hung even in parts and uneven in others. When I finished, I dipped in the water again to rinse off the stray follicles and dried myself off, marveling at how quick it was to towel-dry my hair. If I had some gel, I could've been a straight up rock star. I grinned at my reflection, unable to stop from admiring the stark difference the shorter look had on my whole appearance.

This was a new start. This was a good thing. I would make it a good thing, so help me. There had been too much bad as it was.

Erika slipped the red dress over my head, befuddled when I kissed her cheek. "You look happier than I've ever seen you. Why? Your hair is gone!"

I ran my fingers through my tight curls, grinning at the lightness I felt all over my body. I kissed her other cheek, cheering her up as we walked back to the house. The servants regarded me with pity, some even looking away from my amazing new haircut as if they could not handle the horror.

I went back to Foss's room, which was empty. Foss was yelling at Jamie in Jamie's room. My sheets had already been changed and my room swept, all evidence of the assault gone. I grinned and flopped on the crimson sheets, knowing that if my mother could see me now, she'd flip out and say something about a woman's hair being her crowning glory.

Now I'm a rock star. In a renaissance dress. *I'm the shiz.*

"Hey, Moxie," came a voice so dear to me, I nearly jumped out of my skin when I heard it.

The world and everything in it stopped when Jens materialized out of thin air in the middle of my room.

Fifteen.
Jens the Mermaid Slayer

When words finally came to me, my voice was so out of practice that I coughed for like, a solid ten seconds before my throat felt confident enough for the task. "But you're dead!" I rasped.

He leaned against the wall in that casual way he had about him I always found sexy. "Why does everyone keep saying that?" His dimpled grin found me and breathed new life into my soul that had been flat lined since I left Nøkken. "Do you people really have that little faith in my ability to be awesome? You've seen me kill a Were and off those trolls, but you think a few mermen'll slow me down?" He considered this, waving one hand in the air as he spoke. The motion was mesmerizing. "Well, they did slow me down, technically. But to jump to the conclusion that I died? Shameful. You've seen The Little Mermaid. I'm scarier than them."

I stood, my breath quickening as I took him in from boot to messy black hair, hoping beyond all I was that he was not a mirage conjured up by my rapidly fraying nerves. "We saw you go under and not come back up," I argued. "We saw the big pool of blood around a body that looked like yours. They said, 'fish out the other one'. That was you!"

Jens shrugged. "I guess it wasn't. Might've been the guy I accidentally offed. And by 'accident', I mean it was too easy to be on purpose."

All I could do was stare at him, mouth agape. There he was, in the flesh. This beautiful creature was back from the dead, leaning against my fake husband's wall as if he didn't have a care in the world. I'm sure there was a greeting card for this somewhere, but I was at a loss for words. "I... you... but the blood!"

"Not me." He moved forward, arms still crossed over his chest as he sized me up. He stood in front of me, legs further than shoulder-width apart so he was closer to my height. Jens stared into my eyes and said in his snarky way I'd missed, "You're going to have to get used to the idea that I'm not going anywhere. You're stuck with me, Moxie Kincaid." He ran his hand from my shoulder to my elbow. "Foxy Moxie in this dress." His nose crinkled. "Give me a minute. I can think of something better."

"Shut up," I ordered. I stood up on my toes, closing the gap between us. I was not willing to believe he was real until I tasted his mouth. Our long-awaited kiss was beautiful and painful and warm and slow. We melted in each other's arms. The stoicism, the snark, the violence, the brave fronts – all of it evaporated as we fell back into the rhythm only we understood.

The heat built from the embers of my confusion

and transformed into a fire fueled by desperation. I had to convince myself he was real, that it wasn't a dream now or one long nightmare I'd been living up until this point.

"Shh," he cooed between my frantic kisses. "Hey, it's okay. I'm back."

"You don't understand," I breathed as I deepened the kiss, gently introducing my tongue to his. He moaned, and my body began to hum. "You don't know what I've been through here." I sucked on his lower lip like it was a piece of delicious candy. He smelled like sugar and tasted even better. I hadn't felt Jamie's swell of happiness; our bond was marginally muted by the lingering Gar in his system.

"Tell me." He broke the kiss, breathing heavily as he stepped back. I noticed a solitary sparkle above his upper lip, and wondered how much lavender powder he needed to keep himself afloat. "Tell me what happened. Jamie's been useless for information since he got an eyeful of Britt. Foss told me as much as he knows, but he said you went on a hunger strike and took up a vow of silence when you got on the island?"

"Don't ever do that to me again! I can't lose another person I love. I just can't. That was a stupid thing, to split up like that. Never again! And I just stood there and let it happen, but I knew it was a bad plan! We aren't supposed to be apart, Jens."

He delivered one slow and meaningful kiss, holding my face even after he pulled away. "That you love me? It's a heady thing. I never thought I'd actually get to be with you."

"Don't die, then. Never ever die. Not even playing

Tekken. I can't take it."

He held up his hand to heaven and promised, "As you wish it, I will never ever die. I'll live to be seven hundred million years old, at least. But I suck at Tekken, so I make no promises there. Linus took me to the mat every time." He pressed his forehead to mine and calmed his sarcasm for his best attempt at a serious moment. "But that means you can't stop eating and living. You have to try to survive. For me, if no one else. You think you need me?" He shook his head against mine. "I need you."

I nodded, and I could feel him relax as his shoulders lowered a few inches. I could see in his disquiet that he was worried about me. He'd been through who knows what to get here, but he was most concerned about me. That's the thing about a man worth keeping.

We sat down on the bed together. Jens leaned his elbows on his knees next to me, gearing up for whatever he'd missed. "Now, talk."

Sixteen.
Nik Wilkes Booth

"Wait here," Jens ordered, stomping toward the door.

"Jens, calm down. We're never going to get through me telling you what you missed if you fly off the handle every time you hear something upsetting."

He turned, incredulous. "He molested you! Now if you'll excuse me, I'm going to go collect that Olaf guy's hands. Let him try that again." His jaw was tense, along with every other muscle. He was wound up like a spring and ready for a fight. "And Foss kissing you? I understand the stuff you have to do for show, but I think I have a right to black his other eye for the stuff he did in private."

I sighed, wondering if telling Jens the truth had been the best route. "Look, it was both of us. I was drunk on accident, and Foss was all mixed up because of the fiddle music. You can't black his eye for that. Otherwise you'll have to black mine, too, because I'm just as much responsible."

He stood in the middle of the room, and I could feel his internal debate at wanting to go after Foss. Finally, he exhaled a portion of his anger. "Fine. Fiddles and Gar can make you crazy. I'd be lying if I said I didn't have a ton of regrets from both those things. It didn't go any farther?"

"Of course not. And I told you about it first thing. I'm not trying to hide anything. We weren't ourselves."

"Yeah, okay. I'm actually impressed all you did was kiss. This one time a while back, I was helping Foss out with a few thieves and accidentally..." He shook his head. "Never mind. You don't need to hear that." He postured again, the urge to fight returning. "But Olaf? He signed his death warrant assaulting you."

I shook my head. "I appreciate the thought, but you're supposed to be flying under the radar so you're not suspect when yet another portal gets destroyed."

His frustration turned on me, and despite his childishness, I grinned. It was just so great to fight with him again. His fists clenched at his sides as he fumed. "I can do it without being seen, you know. You can't tell me things like that and expect me to do nothing. You know that's not me."

"I have to be able to talk to you without waking the beast. Newsflash, it's been a downhill mudslide the entire time. Pace your murderous tendencies and pick your favorite bad guy when the story's over." I moved over to him and held his hand, leading him back to the bed. I sat down, but he stood in front of me.

"I hate seeing his ring on your neck. I know it's fake, and I get why he did it, but I hate seeing you parade around as someone else's wife. I wish I could give you something that was more than that. Something that meant more."

"It's not a competition. Foss and I hate each other. He kept me alive and safe. Be grateful. And for the record, he hates seeing his ring on my neck, too. I hate that it's here. We're all pretty miserable."

"Well, that helps a little. And he hasn't kept you safe. I saw what that girl did to you." He looked away, as if the charcoal was still marking my face.

"You can thank Jamie for that, if you're passing blame around. He got stone drunk. If I hadn't passed out, it wouldn't have happened. That wasn't Foss. He can't babysit me all the time. He was trying to figure out the portal thing, which is more important than my hair."

Jens cracked a smile. "It is a sexy haircut, I'll admit. Loved it long, but this? It's grabbable hair. Very sexy."

"Grabbable?"

"Yeah. You know, like this." He kissed me, leaning me back on the bed so he could hover over my body. His fingers wound in the tresses, clenched into a fist and gently pulled. My back arched of its own volition, and his other arm slid to the small of my back. "Absolutely grabbable," he confirmed against my lips. I could feel him trying to kiss the Foss out of me.

"Anything that gets you to kiss me like that," I sighed dreamily.

He glanced down at my neck and frowned. "I still hate his ring on you."

"How can you be thinking about that right now? I'm all aflutter, and you're pissed about meaningless jewelry."

"Aflutter, huh?" He rolled off me onto the bed and stared at the ceiling, his hand resting on his belly. "It's not meaningless. It's like he peed all over you. Do you even know what he went through to get that thing? It's not like he gave you an engagement ring. It's like he gave you a fourth of a country." Then he mumbled under his breath, "And his dick."

I picked up the ring on the string and frowned at it, wondering if I'd see something more than just dollar worth on a leash this time. "Well, I'll give it back as soon as we leave Fossegrim. Honestly, Jens, it's like one of the few nice things he did, and he really didn't want to do it. He said he was doing it for you because he owed you for killing more of the trolls than he did or something."

Jens rolled his eyes. "Oh, brother. And I hate that you're sticking up for him. Makes me almost feel bad I blacked his eye."

I gasped. "Jens! Officially, I'm indignant you struck him, but secretly, I'm fine with it. He needed to be taken down a peg. Macho jerk." I fingered the ring. "But if he asks, tell him I gave you one of these." I mimed throwing a fit with my fists in the air and plenty of head-shaking.

"Will do. Too bad Britta and I are going invisible here. The less people put together, the more chance we have at taking the other portals down." He rolled onto his side and kissed my lips just once, as if to remind himself I was real. I needed the reminder, too. Beneath the bravado, I could tell he had been more worried than he let on. He sighed when he pulled back, twining my fingers through his and placing our hands on his stomach. "Jamie's kind of a mess. I knew he loved Britt, obviously, but I didn't know he'd go down like that."

"We thought you were dead and the others were probably imprisoned. It's been pretty bleak. Jamie was holed up in his room until last night. Kinda my fault. I didn't eat, so no matter how much he ate, he kept getting weaker. Though, on the upside, him eating kept me alive. Bonus, I guess."

"Jamie told me that Foss pushed you around. I notice you kept that out of your little half-story. Skirting around the facts in a dress. Nothing but scandal from you."

"Jamie has a fat mouth. And Foss is who he is. You can't really be that surprised. Maybe he'll come around. Maybe not. After the mission, thankfully I won't be around him to see how it all turns out."

Jens stroked the slope of my cheek, sending tiny pinpricks of tenderness through me. "Foss told me about Olaf's bedslave."

I swallowed. "You know, I could go the rest of my life never again hearing that precious little term. It's disgusting. The best word and the worst one mashed together."

"I can't believe she tried to poison him. You did a good thing." He cleared his throat. "Saw her body posted on the property on my way in. You doing okay?"

"'Okay' is a generous assessment."

"Kinda brilliant, you making her drink the poison. But I know you're probably beating yourself up about that, so I won't high-five you."

"Probably best to hold off on that." I sat up

suddenly. "You have the rake, right? What happened down there?"

Jens touched the pouch tied around his neck and ran his hand over his face. "Nik had a plan he didn't clue us in on. That's what happened." He sniffed and rolled onto his back to examine the ceiling again. "I mean, we got into the water without being seen. I took the weed so I could stay underwater longer. Everything's going according to plan. A few guards swam closer when we got to the portal, but it was nothing I couldn't handle. Nik turns around, shakes his head and pushes me away. He took down the portal before they got to him. No one was right on the portal, but they were close enough to grab him after he destroyed it. He dropped the rake when they nabbed him, and I kifed it. Tried to take out a few Nøkken, but when it was clear Nik was dead and they were going to start searching for the rake, I got out of there. I was on the opposite side of the pond from you guys, but I couldn't get there without being heard. Pesta's Mouthpiece is like a friggin' bloodhound, so I didn't want to risk it. By the time I met up with Britt, you guys were already gone. Took a while for them to open the docks again, but as soon as they did, we ganked the first boat over."

"Everyone's okay? Everyone's here?"

"No, babe. Nik's dead."

I felt so stupid and insensitive. My favorite Nøkken would never again entertain me with his amazing tales of daring feats. "Yeah. I saw his body."

"He knew what he was doing, too. Saved my life and got himself found out. Good news is they think they captured the guy who's been tearing down the portals, so they won't be expecting us at the next stop. I think that was his plan. Bad news is that he's dead. I think he planned on not making it out alive. And now his name's ruined. And all those stories he made up so people would believe he was amazing are wasted." Jens rolled onto his side and stared at my messy curls, deep in thought. "He's not Nik the Man of Valor. He's John Wilkes Booth."

Seventeen.
Beds and Boundaries

One day was all I got with Jens before he left again. This time I made my opinion known that we should not split up, but as I suspected, it made no difference.

The chief and Tomas of the Hills showed up with men a hundred strong each. They were all dressed in leather armor, wearing serious expressions like well-trained military men. The chief's men lined the path on the left side from the house to the main road, and Tomas of the Hills had his men lining the right. It was a little terrifying. I could almost hear the patriotic horns blasting the men off for battle, which hopefully would only consist of Foss playing a game of tee-ball with the rake and then taking a jaunty trip back home. I couldn't really picture Foss jaunty, but I wished that for him all the same.

As I walked through the line of men, I heard several involuntary gasps at my short hair. *Whatever.*

Jamie, Mace and Henry Mancini stayed with me on Foss's property while the others were set to go off on their trek to end the portal. The journey to the next stop was back the way we came, so there wasn't a whole lot of good in all of us going. Except that we'd all be together, which was nothing to sneeze at.

While Jens and I shared a passionate farewell in the privacy of Foss's bedroom, my fake hubby and I bumped fists in lieu of a tearful goodbye. Charles had peeled off one more layer of the curse, and I was grateful for the gradient of change in my moody husband's demeanor. Somewhere along the way we'd grown a fragile respect for each other. It was small and weak, but it was there. He stopped calling me rat, and I complied to his wishes around the house much easier when he stopped being such a jerk. He shared his massive bed with Jens and I, since the staff weren't to know Jens was here. Jens spooned me while Foss snuggled his sheathed sword, occasionally studying my tired gaze after Jens fell asleep. A few minutes after I closed my eyes, I felt a thumb trace my cheekbone. I kept my eyes shut tight, feigning sleep so I wouldn't have to admit that I didn't mind Foss's gentle touch.

Our fist bump had been a nice little ritual, but it did not suffice for the staff. They took my lack of public displays of affection as a young, recently deflowered girl in need of encouragement. The tradition of the entire staff seeing the master off took place at the edge of the property at the end of the long line of men in their fight gear. We all waved, which I thought was good enough, but Erika informed me quietly of my role in all this. "Your husband is leaving for two days to make Fossegrimen history! Give him a good kiss to remember you by. Men stray if you don't give them something to come home to."

She shoved me forward, and I could tell Foss also knew what was expected for the staff to respect me while he was gone. I could feel Jens fuming from wherever he was in his invisible state as I walked up to Foss with a "suck it up and get through this" face.

We stared at each other with dread mixed with resolve as I rolled up my sleeves. "Let's do this," I muttered, and Foss nodded with a hesitant gulp. Before I could talk myself out of it, I reached up and yanked the huge man down by his collar and laid one on him.

Of all the things I never wanted to know about Foss, I knew beyond a shadow of a doubt he was an amazing kisser. I blamed my stomach-flip on that. It was simple mechanics, not passion.

I had one hand bunched in his shirt and the other cupping his face. He kept his hands G-rated around my waist and in my hair, for which I was grateful. I could feel his resistance and anger toward me as our mouths fought, as they always did. We both felt the heat of a connection neither of us were willing to look at too closely. Beneath the show there was truth there, though I wished to plug my ears like an obstinate child to block out the things I couldn't take back once said. Beneath our battling lips surfaced a glimmer of... not friendship... certainly not love... but something other than hatred.

When we pulled away after a surprisingly long time, our foreheads rested together as we took a moment to breathe. "I felt nothing," he lied, kissing me once more.

"Absolutely nothing," I confirmed, my voice breathy and filled with everything I couldn't say aloud. "I'd rather kiss Henry Mancini."

He barely got out a "me too" before his lips tasted mine again, letting out a soft moan of lusty desire. His hand cupped my chin, tilting my head just how he liked it. I hated that I knew how he liked to be kissed.

The kiss ended in pitters and patters of little kisses. They were closed-mouth mini gifts of affection, and a complete overindulgence. "Keep Jens safe, okay, darling husband?" I instructed, eyes closed.

Foss nodded. "Thanks for doing that, lovely wife." His eyes were closed, and I could tell he was steadying himself. I took that as a compliment.

For everything he'd done to save my life and the sacrifices he made to assure my safety, I gave him one genuine kiss. Simple and closed-mouth, but sincere. It served as a harbinger of my gratitude, and he seemed to understand the meaning.

"Don't kiss me like that. It makes me hate you less," he ordered.

I chuckled at his scowl, bumping my fist to his to remind him that our fragile alliance had not changed. "Bring me back a souvenir. And tell our mutual friend, *Jennifer*, that one black eye is enough. This one was on me. I kissed you, not the other way around. All for show."

Foss left me with explicit instructions on how to run the household and the various chores that would need watching over. Viggo was to report to me, which was so strange, I made him repeat it.

Foss mounted his horse and trotted next to the

chief, who gave me a solemn bow of his head, which I returned. The men and Britta left, and I was glad the hammering in my heart was starting to calm down. Another portal would fall, and Foss would be fine.

It was a long, but fun day of seeing to the various tasks and adding a few of my own to the list. The staff gave Mace a wide berth, but no one said anything unseemly. They were all so grateful I started talking, I think that was what they chose to focus on.

I sat on the cleaned counter in the kitchen while Brenda finished up her shutdown routine. "Did I do it right?" I asked.

"Do what, Mistress?" She wiped her hands on her apron and ran the stained material over her face to mop up the sweat.

"Today. Is that how Foss would want me to handle business around the house? Did I forget anything?"

"Not a thing, dear. It's good to hear your voice. We had a running bet that the master'd married a mute."

I chuckled. "I think I'm going to turn in."

Brenda kissed my cheeks and wished me a good night's sleep. I was really starting to fit in, and for the first time on Foss's property, I wasn't shrouded in fear.

I walked into the bedroom and found Mace already in bed with Henry Mancini on his chest, enjoying a good ear-scratch. "You look like you had a good day," he observed with a slight smile.

"I did. I'm exhausted, but it's nice to know if the whole becoming a doctor thing doesn't pan out, I can always moonlight as a dictator." I stretched, indicating that it was time for me to take the bed, and him to scram to one of the other rooms designated for guests.

He did not take the hint, but instead patted the space next to him on the bed.

I could only imagine the Hugh Hefner jokes Jens would make right now. Paranoid boy. I shook my head at Mace. "Time for bed, boundaries boy. You get the room across the hall. I get the big bed all to myself."

Mace frowned. "Are you sure that's safe?"

I clicked my fingers at my puppy, who came running. "Henry Mancini can keep watch. I'm actually looking forward to sleeping in the big bed by myself without Foss or Jens taking up the whole thing. Haven't had a good night's sleep in a while."

Mace swung his long legs over the side of the bed and walked toward me. "I can help with that." He pursed his lips together and started his low, multi-toned whistle that drew me in like a hook around my belly.

I lunged at him and put my hand over his mouth before he got out more than a couple notes, shaking my head vehemently. "No, no. I'll sleep like a normal person tonight. No hypnosis necessary." His silver eyes were so weird. I couldn't help but gawk at them as my hand rested over his mouth. "Bed, big brother. I'll see you in the morning."

Mace nodded, his black hair sweeping over his cheekbones. He kissed my nose, and by the way he hovered, I could tell how starved for affection he was. I couldn't imagine a whole life of being ostracized all because of my parentage. I wrapped my arms around his middle and hugged him briefly so he didn't feel too cast aside. But seriously, I hated sharing a bed with Linus, and didn't want to start that trend with Mace, who I was just getting to know.

I shut the door behind him and flopped on the bed with Henry Mancini, making a nice divot in the covers for my puppy and I to build a nest in. The sheets smelled of Foss with a hint of Jens, but I didn't care. I had my dog back, my boyfriend wasn't dead, and the mission to take down the siren who destroyed my family was still on track.

Eighteen.
Acting the Part

They were supposed to be back a couple days after they left, but nearly a week later there was still no sign of Jens and the others. Jamie was getting restless, but at least he was more social. He and Mace spent some time getting to know each other, bonding over making arrows for Jamie's quiver. It didn't dawn on me until then that it actually did matter if Jamie got along with my new family member, since the prince and I were stuck with each other.

Brenda motioned me into the kitchen, where Viggo was waiting for me. He greeted me with a bow, which I knew I'd never get used to. "Miss Lucy, Master Foss is taking longer than expected to return, and we're running low on a few things around the property. With your permission, I'd like to go into town and purchase what we need."

I shrugged, and then it dawned on me that he needed my blessing to even leave the property. "Sure,

V. Do you need anything from me?"

He dimpled at the nickname. "Only to know if you would like anything added to the list."

"Um, well, I noticed Foss's boots are wearing kinda thin around the toes and the soles. Is that normal? Or does he need a new pair and is too stubborn to admit the ones he's got need to be tossed?"

Viggo looked down on me with appreciation. "Excellent. I'll make sure to pick up a pair for him. If you can get him to actually give up his old boots for the new ones, I'll believe you're the siren everyone says you are."

"Look at you, being a good wife," Mace teased. He and Jamie were red-faced from corralling the horses outside. "Foss is a lucky man."

"Indeed," Jamie joked, donning the only relaxed smile I'd seen on him in days. "This is your chance to get whatever you've always wanted, Lucy. Foss is quite wealthy."

I grinned, tapping my fingers together as I plotted. "I noticed there're no window dressings in his room, just shutters. Perhaps something in pink? Nice and frilly."

Viggo shook his head. "I'm certain he'll have something to say about that."

"Would that thing be, 'Lucy darling, those curtains were the one thing missing from my life. Now that my room is all pink, I can let loose my feminine side. Brenda, make me a red dress in my size, so I can match my beautiful wife.'" I clasped my hands together. "Oo! Can you get underwear in his size dyed pink? He super needs those."

Mocking the master was a scandalous thing for the servants, but since I was the one doing it, they relished in the laughter, as if the joke were something delicious and dangerous to partake of.

I nodded, firm in my rule. "Pink curtains, at least. The girlier, the better."

The day passed much like the others, and I was actually beginning to relax in Foss's house. With each day, I became more comfortable with the routine.

On the tenth day, however, I was getting worried. I put on a smile for the staff during dinner. I'd had to force Jamie out of his room, not willing to let him slip back into his depression and distance.

Mace did his usual song and dance of lurking around my room until I kicked him out. It was sweet, but I knew Jens would throw a fit. Plus, I was in love with the giant mattress for just me and Henry Mancini.

Erika stoked the fire for me and unpinned my hair, which she'd fastened up so it gave the appearance I had buckets of tresses, but just pinned back. She'd helped me get dressed for bed, since apparently, that was something that required two people. I wore a red nightgown that was fitted around my breasts, but hung loose to the floor with capped sleeves that were, let's face it, totally cute.

Erika bundled up my dress from the day to wash when she did laundry next. "You poor thing. Newly married, and Master Foss leaves already. He's an important man, but still. Probably not the honeymoon you dreamed of."

"Total bummer." I tried to look sad, but it was a bad act. I was too comfortable on the huge mattress. It had to have been a California king size, at least.

She sat on the edge of my bed with a conspiratorial air about her as I laid back on the pillow. "Do you think he got you pregnant?"

And just like that, I was wide awake. I sat up and subconsciously touched my stomach. "Probably not. No. Maybe when he gets back." The feigned sadness was stretching it.

"I know he wants an heir. He'll try and get you pregnant right away. I'm certain of it. Maybe then he'd pick up his fiddle."

I swallowed, keeping Foss's secret about his mother tucked tight inside me. "Foss doesn't play, huh?"

Erika lowered her voice. "Oh, he has a fiddle, but he doesn't play it. The Fossegrimen curse runs deep in the master. He doesn't like feeling... Well, he doesn't like feeling anything at all. That's why you being here is so miraculous. I bet you'll have him fiddling away in no time. Perhaps a son would give him reason to play."

I stretched and yawned dramatically before Foss Jr. had a chance to haunt my dreams.

"Oh, listen to me, prattling on. I'm sure you're exhausted. Do you need anything else before I turn in?"

"Nope. You're a gem. Thanks for everything today."

Erika grinned. "For the last time, you don't have to thank me for every little thing. This is what I'm supposed to do. You're actually letting me off easy."

I laid down and pulled the red blanket up to my waist, snuggling Henry Mancini to my bosom. "Night, E."

She bowed, but I heard her whisper, "Goodnight, Mistress L."

I drifted off a few minutes later with a smile on my face.

Nineteen.
Ablaze

The room was warmer than I remembered when noises outside woke me sometime in the middle of the night. I looked out the window and saw a tiny light flutter by. I smiled sleepily when I recognized the butterfly wings of the *eld fjräril*. So pretty. I recalled the chief saying something about them being attracted to fire, and I wondered if Viggo had started up a bonfire in the clearing.

Henry Mancini started barking and nipping at my hand. "Ouch! Careful, buddy." I rolled from my side to my back and looked up at the ceiling as distant shouts filtered in and brought coherence to my hazy thoughts.

There were horses riding around and men shouting. I bolted upright and noticed smoke coming in from under the door. I ran to the window, watching in horror as men from Olaf's camp rode around the property on their black horses. They carried torches and were setting fire to the crops. One touch, and the vineyard was ablaze, the spark traveling so fast, I could scarcely make sense of it.

The wood floor was heating up, and I wasn't sure where the fire was at in the house. I slipped on my gold sandals, scooped up Henry Mancini and ran to the door, grabbing the handle with my gown.

The fire was coming from the front of the house. The walls near the front entrance were covered in orange and white as the house began to burn. I screamed and ran to Mace's room, banging it open and yelling for him to get outside. Jamie met me at the door, terror washing over him as the new reality set in.

People react in all sorts of ways in times of extreme danger. When I get too sad, I shut down. Apparently, when my house is on fire, my mind works like a freaking ninja.

"Jamie! Grab your bow and arrow and get outside! Go invisible and pick off Olaf's men as fast as you can." When he looked like he could not understand his own name, I shouted. "Now, Jamie! Run!"

Mace met us in the hallway, looking around the house in confusion. His eyes landed on me and widened. "The servants' entrance in the back!" he called, grabbing his pack and bolting toward me. He took a struggling Henry Mancini from my arms and ran after Jamie out back.

In the fog of confusion and fear, my eyes fell from the fire on the wall of the front of the house to the floor. Orange and white licked the wood like so many zealous tongues. All that Foss had worked so hard for was bedecked in heat and dangerous light. I took a step toward the inferno, entranced for the moment beyond my capabilities to make rational decisions.

Then I saw it. There, in the middle of the dining room, wrapped in a blanket was Foss.

The moment it registered he was there, the blanket caught on fire. "No!" I screamed.

I forgot about my safety and ran past the blazing red tapestries to Foss. His mouth had blood trickling out of it, and I could tell he'd been on the business end of a bad beating, but until I was sure he was dead, I would not leave him in the house like this.

Stop. Drop. Roll. Stop. Drop. Roll. Thank you, Fire Department people that visited us in school. I got on my knees and rolled Foss away from the blaze until the fire on his blanket was extinguished. Then I unraveled him from the blanket, revealing so many large cuts and bruises on his naked torso, I didn't know where to grab him.

Foss coughed as the fire crept around the dining room, building our own personal inferno, proving that at least for now, he was alive. I grabbed him under the armpits and dragged him to the hallway entrance that was now a ring of fire.

I can't explain how I was able to drag a man of Foss's size out of the encroaching blaze, but I managed it just before the circle closed in and trapped us in the dining room. I tugged and grunted with all my might, and managed to heft him halfway down the hall before the flames realized they'd been remiss in their duty to follow me wherever I went. Orange danced on the top quarter of the walls on either side of me, creeping to the ceiling and climbing slowly down the wall toward us.

Foss opened his eyes and shouted his physical and

emotional pain. "No!"

I tugged as hard as I could, but my pace was pitiful. I'd never fully appreciated how big he was until I was in charge of moving him to safety, which at the moment seemed miles and miles away.

"Leave me!" Foss called in anguish. "Let me burn with my house!" I could tell this was not an attempt to save my life. I recognized losing the will to live in a heartbeat, as it was so close to what mine had been when I lost my family.

"Get up!" I urged. "I don't know if I can get you out before it all goes up in smoke. Please, Foss! Get up!" I continued to drag Foss, but the flames on the ceiling were heating the hallway so much; Foss felt hot to the touch without his shirt on.

I heard an ominous creaking overhead. One of the sconces was ablaze and pulling away from the top of the wall. I yanked and tugged, but I knew I could not pull Foss out of the way in time. Without really thinking it all the way through, I dropped Foss and threw my body over his.

"Lucy, no!" Foss bellowed into my belly, the red fabric muffling his protest.

I screamed when the heavy wooden sconce sliced through the air and cracked me on the small of my back before sliding off me. It would have cut Foss across the neck, doing some real damage for sure.

I could feel that my gown was on fire, so I threw myself backward and smothered it in seconds. It burned my flesh, but I decided to worry about that later. There would be plenty of time to feel pain once we got to safety. "Get up! Foss, try to walk! I'll never get us both out in time!"

He shook his head. "Save yourself, you stupid girl! I've got nothing left!"

I pulled at him with all my might, the burn on my back impeding my burst of gorilla-like strength. "I won't leave without you, so either we both get out, or we both die in here!"

Charles tore back inside for me, terrified when he saw the fire almost completely painting down the walls on either side of me. "Lucy, run!"

Relief like I'd never known flooded through me. "Foss is hurt! Mace, use your water and start putting out the flames! Help!"

"Lucy, I don't have enough in me to put out a fire this big. I can only control water. I can't create it! You have to go now!"

Mace, beautiful Mace grabbed under one of Foss's shoulders and towed him with me the rest of the way. With his help, it was easy to drag him down the hall, then through a second corridor and down the two stairs that led outside.

The night air was like a punch in the face. I looked up and saw the shed was on fire. I heard a sound so horrible, I instantly was drenched in a new downpour of alarm.

Voices. The servants were trapped inside. I saw a piece of wood barred across the double handles and opened my mouth to scream.

Mace's hand went over my mouth and pointed to Olaf's men on horses. They had not seen us from their distance, and that was our only advantage.

One man fell off his horse with an arrow in his

neck. I tracked the trajectory of the weapon and located the invisible Jamie. I shoved Mace's hand away from my mouth. "Mace, can you shoot a bow and arrow?"

"Not as well as Jamie, but yeah."

"Come on, then!" I yanked on his sleeve and ran to Jamie, touching his back when I reached him so I would disappear from view.

"Get to the boats!" Jamie ordered, aiming an arrow and sinking it into another evil man. "I can hold them off long enough for you to escape, I think."

"We're not leaving the servants to burn like that! Give Mace your bow, and you stay invisible and unlock the shed." Then an idea occurred to me. "Mace, can you do your whistle thing and tell the horses to run far away or something?"

Mace's eyes darted from side to side, counting up the animals as Jamie shoved the bow and quiver into his arms. Jamie took off toward the barn, leaving Mace and I exposed. We hid behind the nearest thick tree that had not yet caught on fire.

"I can't control that many animals with so much chaos." He shook his head, his hand wiping his sweating brow. "I'm not even a full Huldra. I don't have it in me."

I cupped his face in my hands and forced him to see me. "Focus, Charles. You can do this, and you have to. If you don't, when the servants bust out of there, Olaf's men'll just slaughter them clean to the ground." I stared into his silver eyes, willing the power of positive thinking into his brain. "Now tell the horses to run south as fast as they can. Tell them to run until they can't run anymore."

Henry Mancini was circling me as he whimpered, so I scooped him up to make sure he didn't run south with the horses. *Jamie! Cover your ears,* I warned. *Charles is going to whistle those horses out of here!*

Mace covered my ears and closed his eyes. He pursed his lips and let loose his most complicated whistle yet. Seven different notes flew out of him simultaneously, wrapping around each other and sending out a message to the horses. I watched around Mace's body as the animals' ears pricked. Despite their masters' commands, they changed direction as one and galloped south away from the property.

"You did it!" I yelled, triumphant.

Mace breathed a gust of relief, pulling me to his chest so he could exhale into my soot-stained hair.

I ran to Foss when Mace released me so he could help Jamie unbolt the door. I knelt by Foss's shoulder and placed my hand on his sweat-soaked chest. "Foss! Where are the others? Jens? Where are they?" I put Henry Mancini down, and he licked Foss's wounds for him.

Foss coughed in my face. "Why didn't you leave me?"

"Where are they?" I repeated, trying to take him with me into the present. I held his cheeks and forced him to look at me. "Olaf's men are gone, but your place is still on fire. You have to tell me where Jens and the others are, so we can get there now."

The look on his face was so sad, I wished I could take the time to comfort him. But there would be days for comforting later. Now was the time to move. When he looked into my eyes, I saw Goliath defeated. It was a thing of heartbreak to watch him so conquered.

"The boats. My fishing boats. They're there now, if they haven't already left. I was supposed to come back and fetch you guys, but Olaf found me."

I smoothed the short hair from his forehead and lifted his head to cradle it. "There. Thank you. See? You saved the day. Now we aren't separated from the group."

"But Viggo. My servants! Olaf's killed everyone in my household but you!"

I glanced up as I ran my fingers down Foss's cheek, resting his head on my lap. "Guess again, pumpkin. Jamie just busted them out of the shed. They're pouring out like ants from an anthill right now." I concentrated on sending Jamie a mental message. *The others are in Foss's fishing boats, so we'll go there. Flag down Viggo and have him take charge. Send them all to the chief's house with word that Foss is dead. He'll take them in. Then come back to me. I can't carry Foss all the way to the docks.*

Jamie answered, *Okay. Is Foss actually dead?*

No, but he's not very alive, either. Olaf needs to believe Foss is out of the picture, or he'll just come back to finish him off. We can't keep going with a tail on us.

Alright. Sit tight. I'll be there to help you with him in a few.

A tear trickled down Foss's face as he watched all he sacrificed and worked for go up in flames. I lifted his torso as much as I could, pulled his shoulders onto my lap and held him.

"You should have left me," he muttered pathetically with such pain in his eyes, I could not look away.

I pressed his temple to my stomach and brushed clumsy fingers through his hair. "Let's not think about that now. Take a minute and say a proper goodbye to your home. We'll figure out the rest later."

Foss reached up and gripped my hand over his chest as we sat together in silence, watching his life burn to ashes.

Twenty.
Branded

Jamie and Mace acted as crutches for Foss. Jamie used his magic to turn them all invisible. I walked ahead holding Henry Mancini and trying to push out all the bad things until I was at a place where I could have a good breakdown. As it was, the pain in my back and other parts of me I had not realized I'd injured began to seep into my consciousness as we walked through the back roads toward the docks.

Walking was a struggle for all of us. Too much smoke had been inhaled. Even Henry Mancini kept his barks to a minimum. I was banged up pretty good, but it was nothing compared to Foss. He was nursing his side and his left leg, hobbling unsteadily and gritting his teeth through every step.

When we reached a well in a rural area, Jamie drew up a bucket of water for us. Now that Mace had a water source nearby, he could use his gift at will. He showered a trickle from his hands over Foss, washing away some of the sweat and streaking black lines of soot over his hard and bruised body. Water was tipped to his trembling lips, and as he guzzled it down, I could see the effort this cost him.

Mace hosed himself down, and then shot out water at Jamie, who was not nearly as filthy. He was injured in various places, though. Jamie had a trickle of blood from his nose, a burn on his back and several score marks on his arms and legs. I wondered how he acquired them all if he was at a safe distance shooting arrows.

I was taking a break sitting on the grass next to Foss's outstretched form. He was a giant compared to me, but even in the shroud of darkness, I could see his utter devastation at losing everything he owned. I wanted to offer him some semblance of comfort, but I'd been in his boat, and I knew there was no solace to be had in such a situation.

I did not realize how dirty I was until Mace trickled water down over my head. Rivulets of black and red streaked down my body and my nightgown. My beautiful gown was so stained and torn, it was beyond redemption.

Mace knelt down at my side and did something so tender, it almost made me acknowledge the horror we'd just endured. Almost. His long fingers tangled in my hair and washed it, massaging my scalp with the greatest care. My coping skills were top-notch, so I shoved down any freaking out over the fire and scheduled my meltdown for another day five years from now when I had plenty of tissues, space and the hard leather of a therapist's couch. For now, I let Mace take care of me as I would him, if I had his powers.

Instead of spraying the water out at me like a shower, as he had for the others, he traced his fingers over my scalp and across my face.

"How'd you get a bloody nose?" he asked with a look of grave concern.

I touched my upper lip and found a trickle of red. "Huh. No idea. I don't even feel it." Henry Mancini licked my toes, and I loved him for not shying away from my smoke stink.

"Well, I do," Jamie said. He wrung out his shirt and shoved the tail of it in the waist of his pants so it hung down across the back of his legs. He pointed to the burn marks all up his arms and a strange divot on his naked chest. "These are all from you dragging Foss out of the house. Not the easiest thing to shoot arrows when I'm laplanded to you."

"Oh, sorry. I forgot about that. But in my defense, our bumps saved Foss's life."

"Which is why I'm not upset," Jamie allowed with a nod of his head to commend my actions. "But this one hurt." He pointed to his chest. "Still stings a little. What is it?" He glanced to my bosom and gasped. "Lucy, the ring!"

"What?" I looked down and let out a muffled yelp. Foss's ring that was hanging on the leather strap around my neck still shined out at the world, despite the soot in the crevices of his engraved crest, but part of the gold was melted over my chest bone. "How do we get it off?" I worried, panicking a little when I pictured a chunk of my skin ripping off with it.

"You really don't feel it?" Jamie asked, itching the sting on his chest.

"I don't feel anything. The adrenaline's still kicking in high gear. Get it off me!" I wanted to claw at it, but knew that was the wrong thing to do.

Mace continued washing me, gently moving his hands over my arms and shoulders. "Let's worry about that when we get on the boat."

Foss resurfaced from his funk next to me and shook his head, sitting up with great effort. "No. We need my ring to buy provisions for the trip back to Elvage. Lucy can go into town and buy what we need using my seal. Even if word's spread that I'm dead, my accounts still have a large stipend left, and she's the lady of the house."

The three men looked at each other to see who should tend to the task. Foss flexed his fingers to test their dexterity and sat up straighter to stretch his back. "Jamie can't do it because the second he starts, he'll feel the tear."

"Tear?" I gulped, looking down at my chest. True, the ring was not touching my breasts, thank goodness, but it was just an inch or two above my cleavage. I wasn't huge into revealing clothes in my normal life when I got to choose what I wore, but it was nice to know the option was there. Depending on the size of the scar, those tank top days might be gone forever. Not a life-altering deal, but a significant bummer nonetheless.

"I'll do it," Foss murmured just as Mace opened his mouth. "You get ready with cold water as soon as it comes off, elf boy," he instructed.

Mace watched my unhappiness with uncertainty. "I can get it off her."

Foss all but growled at my brother. "I'm stronger than everyone here. It's my ring, and she's my wife. My responsibility." He grimaced. "Technically."

"Fine. Whatever. Please just get it off me," I requested, head in hands. "Goodbye, string bikinis. Had I known I had so little time with you, I would've bought you by the barrel," I muttered as I lay down on the grass. Foss hovered over me as much as he could in his battered state. I picked up his hand and moved it over my mouth. "In case I scream," I explained before molding his fingers where they would muffle best. Jamie picked up Henry Mancini, who could sense my distress and had started whining.

When Foss touched the ring, I started to feel the sting Jamie had been talking about. Jamie sat next to my supine body, bracing himself with his hand over his mouth to keep any locals from being alerted to our presence.

Foss worked his finger into the loop, gave it a painful rock back and forth, moving my skin with it. With each jolt, I started to become more aware of my injuries that had been ignored due to my excellent ability to compartmentalize. Foss paused with determination in his eyes and met my anxious gaze with a solemn nod that told me to buck up.

As long as I live, I will remember the feeling of gold being ripped off my skin. I screamed and writhed under Foss, who did his best to quiet my arching back and thrashing head. I shuddered against him, despite my best efforts to toughen up. Miracle of all miracles, he held me tight, and I could not detect a modicum of his usual loathing toward me. Instead he was tender, holding me as I fought my way through the pain and back to his messed up world. "Breathe, just breathe," he urged me, kissing my shoulder as I screamed into his neck and bled on his chest.

Mace was ready and hit the mark with a steady stream of cold water when Foss laid me back on the ground and collapsed next to me. Luckily some splashed onto my face, hopefully disguising the few tears that leaked out as the magnitude of my many injuries slammed into me over and over again.

My arms were burned in several places. Something hot and heavy must have hit my side, because it hurt like crazy when I moved my hips. The small of my back felt like it was on fire still, and something was wrong with my nose. It wasn't broken, but boy, did it hurt. Everything hurt.

Mace cooled my burns and Jamie's until I calmed down and my chest stopped bleeding. I sat up slowly, trying to regain some semblance of composure. Foss tangled his thick fingers in my hair, combing through the wet curls to offer a bit of sweetness to my bleak existence.

"Don't." I batted at his hand and looked away.

"What?" he asked, affronted.

I shook my head, trying to keep the emotion out of my voice. "You'll make me cry. I just can't handle you being nice right now."

"Lucy," Foss scolded me, drawing me back down next to him. He stroked my arm, consoling himself as much as he did me. "You're okay."

"Sure, but you almost died!" Then as quick as the outburst came, I shoved it back down. "I don't want to talk about it." I took several deep breaths before standing, unwilling to look at the damage. It felt like I had a gaping hole fifteen feet wide on my sternum, and I just couldn't deal with seeing it at the moment.

"Let's go," I said, shaking some of the water off me. "We don't want to keep everyone else waiting too long."

Despite my fragile state that threatened to crumble if I examined it too closely, Jamie and I helped Foss to his feet. He was walking a little better after the rest and wash. We trudged on through the night with Jamie keeping the two guys and himself invisible. I felt a little strange walking in front with Henry Mancini and talking with them as we went. I mean, if anyone saw us, I'm sure they would think I was insane. I was soaking wet with a battered body, a singed and torn dress, walking in the dead of night and rambling to myself. Yeah. I'm awesome.

After some indeterminable amount of time, Jamie requested a break when we reached a small pond. "Mace, my chest is burning. Could you hit it with cold water again?" He turned to me. "Lucy, I know you're in pain. You have to say something. It's perfectly acceptable to speak up if your skin is burning."

My fists had been clenched through the pain for some time. "I thought I'd let you whine about it this time. I've been the weakest link for too long. Kinda tired of it."

Jamie shook his head at me and faced Mace, who hit both of us at the same time with his cooling spray. My tension decreased by a million percent, easily. It's amazing how uptight pain can make you.

Jamie fingered his wound tenderly. "Huh. Is that...

Oh, no." He looked over at my chest and laughed. "Jens is not going to be happy when he sees that."

I narrowed my eyes, indignant. "Well, then he doesn't have to look at my breasts if he doesn't want to. It's not like I scarred myself on purpose."

Jamie covered his mouth to stifle his smile. Then both he and Mace chuckled as they ogled my chest. They leaned close to get a good look in the dark, so I shoved them back to remind them I was still a woman. I covered myself with my hands and scowled. "Look, I know this is a boys' club, but you're being gross. And you're my brother. Quit making jokes about my boobs."

Mace blushed through his amusement and waved his hands to excuse himself. "No, no. It's not that, *kära*. I promise. Don't you see it?"

"No. I'm afraid to look. Is it bad?"

Foss looked over at me and his mouth fell open. "Ho! I really don't want another black eye right now."

Despite my unease, I glanced down at my chest. My nose crinkled in confusion as I tried to make out the shape. Squiggly lines and something that looked like a hammer were singed into my sternum. Then it hit me what the design was. Foss's crest was burned onto my skin. Just above my breasts was an indication I'd been married and was now branded for life, even after I gave him back his ring when all this was over.

I whimpered pathetically and wished for a t-shirt. Or a Band-Aid. Actually, if I'm wishing for things, I think I'd rather none of this ever happened. That I was back with my family, playing Tekken with Linus and being an obnoxious winner whenever luck graced me.

I pointed at Jamie, who was still laughing.

"Whatever. You're branded, too."

Jamie shrugged. "Sure, but I'm a large man with hair to cover it over. It doesn't look like anything on me but a little scar. Matches the rest of them. But you're a dainty woman. It sticks out like a beacon. And that is an unfortunate spot, indeed."

I rolled my shoulders back and postured, wearing my mark with pride. "I'm going to choose to forgive you right now because you called me dainty. Let's move, pervs."

I walked ahead of them and tried to ignore their quiet laughter as we stalked on through the night.

Twenty-One.
Due Credit

The dock we landed our small rowboat on when we'd crossed over from Nøkken to Fossegrim was a far distance away from the massive ships used for fishing and trading. Foss owned one enormous pirate-like ship for fishing and several yacht-sized wooden boats for trading overseas. Foss directed us to one of the pirate ships he'd instructed the others to rendezvous at, heaving a sigh of relief when he saw it had not left without us.

It was still dark, but dawn was on the way, so we hurried to the vessel, flagging down Uncle Rick, who looked simultaneously relieved and shocked at my appearance as he lowered the plank for us. "Sweetheart, what happened to you? Come in, come in. Jens!" he called over his shoulder.

The whole loving someone after they've been through the ringer and look like crap thing is something to be admired. Despite my bedraggled state, Jens ran toward me, reaching out his hands and lowering me from the plank down into the boat. I sunk into his embrace and felt myself breathe for the first time in a week and a half. The comfort of his sugary scent and his warm and strong grip on me melted the front I'd been holding myself together with. I burst into embarrassing tears under the last moments of light from their giant red moon, leaving Uncle Rick and Tor to help the others into the ship. Once again, my body stung all over when there was enough support for me to actually feel my injuries again. Jens kissed my face over and over, wiping my tears and holding me upright. When his hand brushed the small of my back, I bit my tongue as Jamie cried out. "Jens! Watch your hands," he barked after greeting Britta. "She's freshly burned everywhere, so maybe just hold her hand or something."

Jens jumped back from me. "I'm sorry, Loos! What happened? What took you guys so long? We were supposed to meet here days ago! We were this close to coming after you."

Foss was lowered to the floor of the gently rocking ship. He held his side, chest heaving as he spoke. "Olaf. It was Olaf. He must've had a tail on me. He sent his men after me, beat me up and took me home. He set my property on fire and left me to burn in it." He coughed and winced, holding his ribs. "We barely got out alive."

Questions and exclamations flooded out at Foss, who was not totally up for answering everything. He held up his hand to stave off the inquisition. "My servants survived and escaped, but my home is gone. Everything was burned." He glanced at me, clearly embarrassed. "Lucy pulled me out of the house before it burned down. She saved my life. Twice, now."

I really had nothing to say to that. When everyone looked at me, I shrugged. "Whatever. Let's get on with whatever the next part of the plan is."

Foss shook his head. "No, Lucy. You saved my life, so this is me paying you back."

"Huh? By what, telling them what happened?"

Foss wrinkled his nose in confusion. "By giving you your due credit."

I can't really explain it, but for some reason, that disgusted me. I walked over to him and towered over his sprawled out body, hands on my hips. "Is that all your life's worth? Pride? You don't know me at all if you think that makes us square. Normally I wouldn't care, but you were terrible to me in the beginning. No. We're not square until you pay me what you think your entire life is worth."

Foss was taken aback. He blinked up at me, mouth open at my sudden gall. "But I don't have anything to give you. I'll be declared dead soon."

I waved my hand to show him he was on the wrong trail, yet again. I made a buzzer sound that I'm pretty sure just confused him more. "Wrong again. I don't want your money. We'll be even when you pay me back for every mean thing you've ever said to me and Britta, and you give me back what you think your life is worth. You owe me. You owe me a new personality from you and more than you're currently capable of giving."

Britta's eyes were wide when I spoke on her behalf. *You're welcome, sista.*

"I don't understand what you want from me.

Thank you for saving my life. After everything I put you through, I'm surprised you didn't let me burn."

I softened. "That's maybe the first sensible thing you've said. I'll let you know when you've paid off your debt to me." I almost called him a rat, but Martin Luther King would have been more gracious. "Now let's do whatever we need to ripcord out of here. Those men were no joke."

Tor was the first to snap back to the present. "Ya heard tha queen. Get Foss down below tha deck so he's not seen. It won't do ta have Olaf's men after our ship. Best let him think he finished tha job."

Foss shook his head. "We need provisions. This ship isn't stocked for long journeys. Lucy, you have to take my ring into town and buy what we need."

"I'll go with her," Jens volunteered. He looked down at me and gripped my hand. "Not out of my sight, Mox."

"Everyone else, down below," Tor ordered. "Except Alrik. Ya've got a face people trust, so ya stay above and make sure no one tries ta light us on fire."

Twenty-Two.
Adapt or Die

Britta dressed the wound on my lower back so I could wear a proper dress, threw my blue gown from Elvage over my head and sent me on my way in a matter of twenty minutes. I still looked like I'd lost a fight with a pillowcase full of batteries, but it was an improvement nonetheless.

The marketplace was visible from the docks, which gave me just enough tether to leave my laplanded buddy on the boat so he could rest.

Jens was invisible as he walked behind me, whispering funny or crude things over my shoulder as we made our way to the marketplace. Commerce was just beginning to stir at the first sight of the sun on the horizon. He directed me to the different booths and told me what to order. Some of the things I could carry, but others had to be delivered. I paid probably too much extra to have them delivered immediately, waiting at the booth until I verified someone left with the goods to place in Foss's ship with Alrik to sign for it, or however they did things like that here. I really missed the internet, and knew I could secure all these things with a few easy clicks.

I bought too much food, a few dresses for me and Britta, and new clothes for the guys, all except Tor. They didn't sell dwarf clothing anywhere I saw. He'd just have to love the new axe I had sent to the ship. I purchased an assortment of artillery that Jens instructed me on. Bows and arrow, knives of all sizes and shapes, and a few other weapons I hoped we would never have to use were sent to the ship. I ordered a case of Gar from a vendor I knew Foss liked, dozens of fur blankets, soap, a few hambones for Henry Mancini, and whatever else Jens requested over my shoulder.

My eyes landed on a beaded purple nightgown that I was drawn to magnetically. I flashed Foss's ring and bought the purple one for Britta and a black one for me. Let Jamie try and forget he's in love with her in that. I felt Jens's hand trace my hip, and I shivered.

Foss needed new boots, and I got all the small things he liked that I'd found around the house. His soap, towels, clothing, cheese, and most important of all, a fiddle. They had the garden variety for sale, but when I saw one that had clusters of grapes carved into the sleek body, I knew I had to get it for him. The curves of the instrument were almost sexy, and though I'd never played an instrument before, I wished for the skill.

Most of the merchants did not question my authority over Foss's estate. Word had spread of the "Guldy" Foss had acquired, and they referred to me as such, staring at me as I went. One of the vendors requested I show him Foss's ring to verify the purchase. I heard Jens's strangled whine of fury when he saw Foss's crest branded on my chest. I stepped back and pressed my heel onto his toe to remind him to keep his cool.

"I'm going to murder that man in his sleep," he whispered.

"You'll do no such thing," I said quietly. "It was an accident from the fire. Chill."

We finished up and walked back to the boats with the last delivery man, passing several coming back from the ship on the way. Uncle Rick's eyes were wide at the bounty stacked up in crates all around him. "I guess it's best you never got yourself a credit card," he remarked.

"They didn't have any pink ponies for sale." I did a good "aw shucks" gesture for his amusement. "Foss told me to max out his accounts. I did the best I could, but I didn't even make a dent. Kind of a rush, but when you're thinking someone's going to set your escape vehicle on fire, it takes a little something out of the thrill. Plus, no heels. What's a shopping spree without a decent pair of frivolous high heels?"

"It's the one thing Undra's missing." Jens peeked at my scar as he hopped off the plank and into the ship. He untied the line after verifying we had all our stuff, and we were off.

Jens had instructed me to purchase a few hammocks and set about installing them with Jamie's help. I showed Britta the purple nightgown that really was more modest than most of the dresses Tonya wore, but Britta blushed as she pushed it back into my arms.

"I can't wear that!"

"It's no more racy than the stuff I had to wear," I protested. I looked it over. It wasn't sheer. It was normal dress material that hung to the ground. The only difference was the obvious display of breasts. "You don't have to wear it, but I highly doubt you have enough clothes. You've been switching between that dress and your one from Elvage and the kilt for weeks. Might be nice to have something comfortable to sleep in." I draped it over her shoulder. "Plus, Foss owes you a few good moments for giving you so many bad ones over the course of this trip. He paid for it, so you might as well enjoy it."

Britta looked over the thing of scandal and beauty with trepidation and desire. "I don't know what to say."

"Say you'll wear it and give it lots of use."

"I'll think about it."

I could tell she'd tried it on when we sat down for dinner a few hours later. Her cheeks were pink and she could barely look at Jamie, casting me conspiratorial looks throughout the meal. Half of the group was ravenous; they'd not eaten proper meals on their journey to and from the Fossegrimen portal. We went through quite a bit of the fresh food in one go. I wondered how long the journey would be, and hoped I'd gotten enough supplies for it.

Foss was silent and sullen throughout dinner. He kept his head bowed over his plate and hunched with his elbows on the table. I don't exactly know how it happened, but I'd somehow become the only person he would interact with. When I noticed halfway through the meal that he hadn't touched a bite, I nudged the grump next to me, speaking quietly to him while everyone else carried on lively conversations. "Foss, you should eat something. When was the last time you ate?"

He shrugged. "I'm not hungry."

I placed my hand on his bare back and rubbed soothing circles, taking care not to brush over his many injuries. "The fresh food won't last long, and then it's beef jerky till the cows come home."

He kept his eyes from me and focused on his food. "I hate when you're nice to me."

I sat up straighter. "I don't actually care what you think you hate. Do you care that I think you're a horrible person who isn't capable of real growth? No. We'll get through the rest of the trip however we can. Then when it's over, you'll be rid of me. You can be all kinds of happy then." I took a bite of a tomato and sighed at the purity of the taste. "I have it in my day planner. Destroy portal, be rid of Foss. Step one, step two."

Foss did a silent snort at my humor, but still did not eat.

I picked up my plate and his, nodding toward a spot near the back of the boat. "Come on."

I kissed Jens on the forehead before leading Foss off away from the group. I pointed to a spot where we could eat on the floor and see the ocean. When he sat down, I could tell it cost a great effort.

"You sound like an old man," I commented as Henry Mancini scampered toward me and snuggled onto my lap.

Foss grunted as he shifted next to me, both of us

facing out onto the water.

I handed him his plate and continued eating as I talked, using my dog's back as a table to balance my plate on. "I was never as rich as you are."

"As I was," Foss corrected, staring out at the waves with a hard expression, as if he was daring the ocean to give solace neither of them possessed. "I'm dead now with nothing to my name."

"I didn't have as much to lose, but I understand a little of what you're going through."

He gave me a good "pfft" laced with his superior attitude. "You couldn't possibly."

I settled in for a barrage of his mean behavior and muscled through. "Everything I've ever owned was burned to the ground. My few friends think I'm dead, too. When I get back to my world, I'll start a new life in yet another new place by myself." I considered this, then amended my statement. "Well, with Jens, luckily. Sound like anyone you know?"

Foss stared at me, finally paying attention to something other than his pain. "I didn't know that."

I chewed on another tomato and wished for twenty more. "The things you don't know about the people around you could fill a book. Just because I'm not important to you doesn't mean I'm not important." I sighed, lowering my voice. "I've never had a home to live in for more than half a year. And every time I've had to pick up and leave, the place behind me was cleaned out or burned up. Sometimes it was ordered by Jens, who I didn't know at the time."

Foss said nothing, so I assumed he was still listening. At least he wasn't tearing me down or arguing. Progress.

"I had two awesome parents and a twin brother who was my best friend. I lost them all on the same day. I know twenty isn't as young where you're from, but it's young for my world. I was on my own, and had to make a decision whether I would wither away or climb out of my depression and claw my way back to the world. You have to make that same decision." I picked a grape off my plate and put it in his hand. "You're eating," I commanded gently.

Without considering his stalemate on food, Foss popped the grape into his mouth, and I could see a small amount of life flicker inside of him.

"I know you don't think much of me, but I mattered to exactly three people who I would have died for. Every day without them, I'm a little less. Less fun. Less happy. Just... less." I knew I was treading on dangerous ground, giving the pit bull ammunition, but I trudged onward, knowing he couldn't really get much more surly, ammunition or not. "I'm sorry you lost Kirstie because of me. I didn't mean to make her so mad, honest. I know she made you happy, and I would never want to take that away from you. You didn't seem like you had a whole lot of happy in your life."

Foss ate a second grape without coaxing. "There's more to life than smiling."

"True. I can't imagine there's much of a life without it, though."

"Your world is frivolous," he ruled, spearing a tomato with his fork.

"And your world is mean." I shrugged. "And you can't go back there. You'll start a new life somewhere else. Best learn to adapt."

He nodded, and I took that as a sign that I was finally getting through his thick skull.

"For what it's worth, I'm sorry you lost your home. It was beautiful, and I could tell you worked hard to make it yours. Your servants loved you, though I'm not totally sure why." I ventured a glance in his direction. "You seemed less of a prick there, too."

He did not have anything to say to this, so he huffed at me.

"You don't know much about my world or me, and if we last through Elvage, you'll come with me to the Other Side. I gotta tell you, if you push me around, talk down to people or be your usual charming self, you're likely to get shot if you're in the wrong neighborhood."

"I can handle arrows."

I chuckled. "Oh, lovebug. We have guns, not arrows. Far more deadly. You hit the wrong person, you'll just up and get yourself killed. It's your choice, but I thought you'd like the chance to start over. You all never bothered to explain the different cultures to me, and that sucked. You should know what'll be expected of you."

"I can't imagine I'd do well in your world."

I put down my plate and turned to face him. "Adapt or die, Foss. It doesn't much matter what you want or how you feel you should be able to behave. Adapt or die, starting with not being such a jerk." I touched his hand, not letting him flinch away from me. "You have an opportunity for rebirth here. A chance to change. My advice? Take that chance."

Foss eyed me with skepticism to cover over a heavy

heart. "I liked my life. I don't want to give that up."

I shrugged. "You don't have a choice." I squinted at him. "And I thought you were strong. I adapted in your world. Guess that makes me stronger than you." I took a grape from his plate and popped it in my mouth. "I figured as much."

Foss glared at my thievery and I smiled, knowing that was a sign he still had fight in him. If he had fight, there was a chance he could rise to the occasion and someday be a better person.

"Oh! I forgot. You can have your ring back." I reached for the knot to untie the leather strap.

He placed his large hand over the ring on my sternum. "Keep it until we get over to the Other Side. You and this ship are the only things I still own. Dead or not, my name will help you through Undraland."

My mouth tightened. "I hate you so much. You don't own me. No one owns me."

Foss straightened, his hand still resting on my chest. "I paid for you. Weapons, shoes, clothes, women. I buy it, it makes it mine. I. Own. You."

Henry Mancini sensed my anger and snarled at Foss until he removed his hand from me. My upper lip curled as I flipped through my mental Rolodex of horrible things to say in response. I landed on taking the high road. *Thanks a lot, Martin Luther King.* "Well, I tried. And technically, you're a dead man, so you own nothing. This ship is friggin' mine, oh darling husband. If I was being a jerk, I'd say the ring is mine, too. And your remains, which means, you. So, technically? Technically, I own you." I stood and ruffled his short hair. "Suck on that, princess."

Twenty-Three.
Better Than This

Aside from one "fun family relocation adventure" in the middle of the night once, I'd never been on a boat. Seasickness wasn't a thing I was familiar with, so I spent a decent amount of time in my hammock when I was not needed, nursing my wounds and pretending I wasn't green around the gills with the motion of the churning ocean.

When night fell, Jens hoisted himself into my hammock, and I tried not to ralph all over him. "Ugh. Don't rock me too much. I'm not used to this." He'd slid a bucket next to us that Henry Mancini was sniffing.

Jens scooted his body underneath mine so I could rest on him and have a little stability. "Better?"

"So much. I wish I knew more about boats so I could be useful."

He ran his fingers through my hair. "Once you stop barfing like the adorable little puke machine you are, I'll be sure to put you to work swabbing the deck like a good pirate."

"Thanks, Captain Crunch. What's the bucket for?"

"In case you toss your cookies again." He kissed my blonde tangles. "You're so cute when you're gross."

"Ugh. Don't say cookies." I exhaled contentedly atop his chest. "I miss cookies. I took chocolate chunks for granted. And you smelling like a big old batch of them doesn't help matters. I miss a whole slew of things."

"Me, too. I miss those orange circus peanuts. Undra doesn't have processed food." Henry Mancini curled up under our hammock and Jens lowered his hand to scratch behind his ear.

My nose wrinkled and I groaned. "Oh, no. You're disgusting. And five, apparently. What self-respecting adult actually eats those? I knew you had to have a flaw. Well, at least now I know. Out with it. What else you got?"

He chuckled, and the sound warmed me from my bare toes to the tip of the ear he was tracing with his forefinger. The air coming off the ocean was getting chilly as night fell, but Jens was my warm towel fresh from the dryer. "I taught Linus how to hotwire a car, which is how you learned."

"Then I blame you for the grounding of the decade when we got caught."

"Who do you think turned you in?"

I gasped. "You evil, evil man! We got in so much trouble!"

"Good. You should. You were only fifteen."

I lifted his shirt and placed my cold hand on his stomach, tracing the muscles that tensed as I slowly teased them. "Tell me more about human you."

He stretched the arm that wasn't wrapped around me over his head, hooking his hand under a few of the hammock's loops. "I have a thing for black licorice."

"Now you're just making things up. No one's that nasty."

"Hmm... Let's see. Things about human Jens. That red Partridge Family t-shirt Linus bought you? It was from me. He wanted to get you AC/DC."

"Aw. A commendable second choice."

"I played on the soccer team with Linus during the summer sophomore year. Your parents were worried about him breaking bones, but didn't want to treat him like a sick kid, so I helped keep him from getting hurt."

"Huh? I was at every one of Linus's soccer games. I never saw you."

"No one saw me. I was invisible."

I kissed his cheek. "It's so strange that he knew about you and I didn't. That the whole family did. How could they keep something like that from me? They were all in on it. You two were friends. You hung out and shot the breeze with my parents."

"There was talk about telling you. I wasn't opposed, but your dad didn't want you to know about me. He knew I had a little thing for you and wasn't willing to box you in like that."

"Box me in?"

"Yeah. It's a sports term. It's when one player –"

"I know what it means. I just don't know how that would box me in."

Jens was silent for a minute as he stared up at the wooden overhang that shielded us from the elements. "Think about it. I'm assigned to your family. If we break up, you're still stuck with me. I'd have to watch you be with someone else. Marry some rich tool. Guard him and your kids. It's a lot to take. Your dad wanted me to wait until you were twenty-one to introduce us."

That sure knocked the wind out of my sails. I didn't know what to say to the pressure that put on our relationship, so I stuck with shtick. "I end up with a rich guy, huh?"

"I'm a rich guy. He's a rich tool, just to clarify." He wound his finger around one of my curls. "You're deflecting, which means you're secretly freaking out. Talk."

"Oh, you think you know me so well. As it happens, I was thinking about what color pony I was going to make you buy me for Christmas, Moneybags. I'm leaning towards purple."

"A double deflection? Excellent defense, babe. We don't have to talk about it right now."

"Good." I buried my face in his shirt, inhaling the sugar cookie smell of him that chased away the trout-ish scent of the ocean and the fishing boat. Jens chased away a lot of the things that plagued me. We grew quiet as the boat rocked our little hammock. There had been so much danger and fear; it was odd to have whole minutes strung together that held nothing but peace. "Jens?"

"Yeah, baby?"

"When there's no more danger and Pesta's good and dead, will you still love me like this?"

He gave a short, soundless laugh. "No. I'll love you much better than this. We'll go on actual dates to normal places. We'll have a house, not an apartment, with that white picket fence you've always wanted. We'll have a garden. Not as good as mine in Tonttu, but good enough to brag to the neighbors." He kissed my lips, and I could feel emotion swelling in him. "We'll go to concerts and join a bowling league or something goofy where we get to wear weird shirts but still look totally normal." His fingers laced through mine and he kissed my knuckles. "No, baby. I'll love you much better than sleeping on the ground and letting you live in fear."

I could tell there was more he wanted to say, but I let him keep his secrets. I let him keep me in his arms. I let the waves rock us to sleep. I let myself fall even more in love with my constant protector and most faithful friend.

Twenty-Four.
Farlig Fisk

I woke in the middle of our fourth night at sea to Henry Mancini whining and circling underneath Jens and me. He was sniffing the floor, upset about something. It was impossible to disengage myself from the hammock without waking Jens, so when he stirred, I pressed my body into his and whispered, "Go back to sleep, baby. I'm just getting up to stretch my legs a little."

"Okay. Want me to come with you?" He kissed my lips with his that were slightly swollen from sleep, beckoning me to stay in his arms.

"I'll be back."

"Good. I like you sleeping on me in that nightgown. Sexy." Jens clicked his fingers and whistled once to get Henry Mancini's attention. "Stay on mama, boy."

I smiled when my puppy obeyed and followed after me, nipping at the black fabric that Britta had hemmed so it brushed against my toes. No one had ever referred to me as "mama", and I was glad Jens couldn't see my pink cheeks.

I went for a walk around the boat's... main floor? Deck? Hull? I don't know the nautical terms. Tor was at the helm (I knew that term because Foss had barked at me to stay away from it). My favorite dwarf was looking out onto the never-ending abyss with a scrutinizing stare as he kept an eye on the wheel. "Whatcha doing?" I asked, stretching my arms over my head and twisting my torso to give my spine an invigorating squeeze.

His eyes did not stray from the gentle waves. "It's too peaceful. Too quiet. I don't trust it." He let out a loud fart, but I was so used to him doing that, I didn't even flinch, just made sure to stay upwind.

"I don't do much sailing, but isn't that a good thing?"

He shivered. "I don't sail, neither. Most our work is done underground. If I can't touch tha earth, I'm not happy."

"I feel you."

"Dwarves don't swim. We sink like rocks."

"Very cute rocks, I'm sure." I elbowed him, and he grumbled through his blush.

"I miss dwarf Gar," he admitted.

"Yeah? Is it much different from Foss's?"

He pfft'd at my amateur question. "Only as different as my height is from his, the giant."

I chuckled softly next to him. "If we're talking about missing things, then I'm putting in a vote for indoor plumbing. Wait till you get to the Other Side. It'll blow your mind."

"I miss my home. I don't know how Foss and ya can carry on with no familiar place ta return ta."

"You manage. Not well, but you do." We stood in amicable silence before Henry Mancini grew impatient. He began barking at the sea. "Shh. Baby, you're going to wake up Foss. He's already crabby." I picked up my puppy and stroked his thick gray fur, nuzzling his nose with mine. "Can you imagine him sleep-deprived? Absolute monster." Henry Mancini did not hearken to me. He growled out at the gentle waves. "There's nothing out there," I assured him, though this did not calm him as I'd hoped. To humor my little buddy, I followed his line of vision and froze. "T-tor? What the crap is that?" I pointed with a shaking finger to a scaly protuberance poking out of the water's surface.

Tor's eyes fell on the tentacle that was fatter than he was. It was wider than Foss, even. "No. It can't be. We're not even in his territory!" He turned the wheel to steer us away from the thing that was nearly a soccer field away still. I heard in Tor's tone a fear I was unfamiliar with as he grabbed my arm roughly. "Lucy, wake Foss. Run, girl! Go! Tell him we're staring down a farlig right now!"

I obeyed immediately. By now, I knew better than to ask questions. I ran down the steps to the bottom of the ship with Henry Mancini where Foss was holed up to wait out his sadness. I banged on the door, sensing this was not the time for stalling. "Foss! Wake up!"

When he did not answer, I opened the cabin door and ran to his hammock, shaking him awake.

"What? Get off me, rat!"

Oo, when this was all settled, I'd get him for slipping back to the nickname I loathed. "Tor needs you. He said something about a farlick? Forlug? Something bad. I don't know what it is, but he needs you, stat."

Foss was instantly awake and alert. "A farlig?" He pulled on his pants and then grabbed my arm and shoved me to the back of the small cabin where there was a window looking out just a few inches above sea level. "Did he say farlig fisk?"

I thrust his grip off my bicep. "Quit manhandling me! I hate it!"

He moved Henry Mancini inside with his foot and backed me into the corner, making my heart race. He probably wouldn't try to kill me with Jens on the ship. I was pretty sure. His hands reached out and gripped my shoulders as he pressed my spine to the wall, breathing in my face. "No matter what happens, stay right here until I come and get you. Do you understand?"

I wanted to curse at him, but instead I nodded, not accustomed to the note of fear in his eyes that matched Tor's.

I whimpered when something bumped the boat, knocking us off-balance. "What was that?"

"Stay here!" he repeated, banging the door shut behind him before I could get out another question. I went to the window and looked out on the darkness to try and make out the slithery shapes that swam by in the abyss.

I heard Jens and Jamie shouting, followed by a loud whistle from Mace that I had to cover my ears against, in case it would make me do something crazy like jump into the water or something.

I didn't understand the danger. All I saw was the water's surface until another tentacle the size of a tree trunk stretched out of the sea and landed across the boat, knocking me to the floor. I snatched at Henry Mancini, who was one giant sea monster away from losing his mind. I muffled my scream in his fur as all the stupid horror movies Linus used to make me watch about sharks eating people and crazy monsters in the ocean flooded my brain. They always ended bloody, and the virgin died in every horror movie I'd ever had to sit through.

The cabin door slammed open, and I screamed.

"It's just me!" Britta called, and then shut the door tight behind her. She ran to my corner and threw herself on me and Henry Mancini, crying and shaking with terror I'd never seen on her. "We're going to die! We're all going to die!"

We clung to each other in the dark in our matching nightgowns, letting our fear loose in the privacy of the cabin. Muting our reactions to everything for the sake of not appearing to be the weakest link was taxing, and the buildup had led to an emotional explosion from Britta that spread to me and festered until my tear ducts were also overflowing with every violent jerk of the ship. Her hair fell around us in brown waves, giving some cover to hide behind in case the monster took a peek inside the tiny window.

Some invisible force whacked me across the face, knocking my head to the wall. "Ouch!" I blinked away the sting as Britta held my cranium and checked for blood. "What the smack?"

"It must be Jamie!" she exclaimed, turning for the door and making to stand.

"No, Britt! You stay here. If they sent you down here, they have their reasons. Stay put. Am I bleeding? If I am, you have to stop it. We can't have Jamie passing out up there."

Britta nodded and gulped down her terror, examining my head with shaking fingers. "I don't see any blood." She exhaled a small amount of her dread for Jamie's plight, letting the steam off the top so she could think clearer. "I'm sorry. I've never seen a farlig before. It's so much bigger than the legends!"

"Don't be sorry. You're allowed to have a good freak-out." We slid to the floor and Britta collapsed in my arms. I brought her head to my bosom, patting her hair and shushing her like a mother would until she found herself again. She was so beautiful with her hair down, crimped from her nearly permanent braids. "What's out there, Britt? What's a farlig?"

Britta spoke in a wavering voice through her tears. "Farlig fisk. It's a sea monster with tentacles sixteen meters long and a body taller than three houses! But it's not supposed to be in these waters. It lives way out in the eastern end of the ocean. Only experienced fishermen ever come close to it, and most never live to tell the tale. It's not supposed to be on this pass! Fossegrim to Elvage is a common route! That he's here's a curse, for certain!"

"Okay, okay. Calm down. What kind of a monster is it? Like an octopus?"

Britta nodded into my chest. "An octopus with

dozens of legs and a body like a squid with a giant mouth and eyes. It lives on fish, but it tears apart boats and swallows us, too!"

My stomach churned. "Sixteen meters long? That's... that's a sizeable guy." I didn't have much room to lose my mind so far on this journey, but that nearly tipped it. I took a steadying breath. What was a giant sea monster compared to spider kittens who tried to lay their babies in my spine? Or Werebears that targeted me even in suburban areas? All of it piled onto the filter of things I'd properly throw a fit about later, once I could process the whole of Undraland. As it was, every time I turned a corner, it seemed a new terrifying creature was waiting to pounce. Yes, my scheduled freak-out on the therapist's couch in five years would be a doozy.

The ocean tossed us, and we were ill-prepared. Britta, Henry Mancini and I were flung across the cabin and smacked into the wall.

Jamie's voice boomed in my brain. *Lucy, stop! You must be more careful. We're dying up here, and I can't be distracted by the link right now.*

I'm sorry! I answered Jamie. "Britt, you have to help tie me down somehow. When I get hit down here, it distracts Jamie up there." I cast around for something to secure myself with.

"Get in Foss's hammock," she suggested. "If you hold onto it, the most you'll do is rock."

"Good plan. Hold onto Henry Mancini for me, then." Britta picked up my puppy, who was alternating between barking and crying. I understood his emotional plight. My bite was usually seconds away from a good tearful breakdown, too. I hoisted myself onto the hammock and clung to the netting. "You get in here with me!" I urged, watching her brace herself unsuccessfully against the rocking of the ship.

Britta handed me Henry Mancini and climbed in just before another ominous *thunk* hit the ship. We gripped the netting and each other, sandwiching my puppy in between us. She was a good foot taller than me, which only made me feel more childlike and helpless.

The boat that had not so long ago ridden along on gentle waves was now tipping and rocking from the tidal wave the monster set off with his crazy huge body.

Britta's anxiety took on the form of a confession, using me as her priest. "One time, I stole a whole bushel of pears from my neighbor's trees. He was away, and they were falling off the tree! I canned them and saved them for him, but I only gave him half what I made and kept the rest for myself! I'm a horrible person!" she blubbered.

"Ah!" I arched against Britta as something hard scraped across my back. I writhed in the hammock to get away from it, but it was Jamie's injury that imprinted itself on me. Britta tore my dress up to my ribs and rolled me on my stomach to examine my back. "Is it bad? It feels deep. Oh! It stings!"

Britta cried out and jumped off the hammock, picking up Foss's shirt and dabbing my back with it as she sobbed. "It'll be alright, little sister. It'll stop bleeding. I can stop it!" her voice was nearing hysterical, which did not give me much solace.

It dawned on me that if Jamie was tossed

overboard, I would be dead in minutes. I tried to center myself and not feel the burning on my back or the fear in my heart. Henry Mancini began licking the blood off me, which was too gross for me to handle. "No, no, baby. Don't do that. Let's not go out like savages."

"The farlig had yellow eyes, Lucy!" Britta mourned as she dabbed at my back. "Yellow eyes and was foaming at the mouth. I've never seen one before, but in all the stories I've heard, they've had black eyes."

My stomach sank. "You don't mean... Pesta couldn't have possessed that thing, could she? It's enormous!"

Britta nodded, squealing when the boat dislodged her footing and made her fall on her butt. She scrambled back into the hammock and held on for dear life, pressing the coarse fabric of Foss's shirt into my wounds. "The Mouthpiece fears the Fossegrimens because they hate Pesta for bringing a curse down upon them. He would never set foot on their soil. Of course Pesta would send a soul to torment us!"

Then something knocked me in the back of the head, causing me to cry out again. "Ow! Ow, ow, ow, ow!" There was a weight on my chest that threatened to crush me, which was hard to articulate to Britta. When it was lifted, I gasped and felt my ribs to make sure nothing was broken. "I hate this stupid bond!" I yelled.

Britta patted my naked back with Foss's wadded-up shirt. "There, there. You're both still alive. He must be fighting valiantly up there."

Yes, your boyfriend's amazing, and I'll pay the price for it. I started wishing Jamie was less heroic and more of a coward when danger reared its ugly squid head.

In my reprieve between psychic injuries, I wished beyond all hope that I could do something to stop the farlig. Biting down on the rope netting to brace myself for the next attack, I yearned for a distraction. "Talk to me, Britt. Make me not think of what's out there."

Britta nodded. "I once told on Jens to our parents when he and Jamie stole Gar from Jamie's father's cellar."

My laugh mutated into a scream when something sharp stuck me in the thigh. I could feel ribbons of blood running over the skin and dripping onto the floor below.

Henry Mancini licked my face and whined. I tried to give him a brave smile, but both of us knew it was a bad acting job.

Britta's voice was high-pitched due to stress, and she rattled off more to distract me, the golden lovebug. "And another time, I dipped Helsa's favorite dress in lye, rolled it in salt and let it dry out in the sun because she was calling me an old maid. I was so upset, but I shouldn't have done that!"

"Is that the chick who dumped water on me? Well, she deserved it. You're absolved."

"If only."

Another something bashed me in the shoulder. I choked back the cry so Britta didn't have a panic attack, and then set my mind into overdrive trying to think of an idea to fish us out of this mess.

Twenty-Five.
Chemistry Lessons

It was an entire minute of intense racking my brain before anything clicked in my mind. I rolled over and shot up on the hammock. "Britta! How does Foss clean the outside of the boat?"

She answered too slowly for my liking. "There are barrels of cleaner down below the deck."

My heart pounded in my ears. "And the cups and silverware, are they aluminum?"

"Yes. I think so."

"You think or you know?" I demanded, gripping her shoulders and staring into her eyes like a crazy person.

"Yes, they're aluminum."

"The cleaner. Does it have lye in it?"

"Of course."

I kissed her cheeks hard and tumbled off the hammock. "You beautiful girl! That's it! You up for taking out the sea monster, or are we gonna let the boys have all the fun?" I leapt to my feet with new purpose, ready to take on the world.

Britta nodded her assent, but she was terrified now of the monster and of my determination. "But we're supposed to stay put."

"We'll die down here, and you know it. If you're in, run and grab me as many barrels of cleaner as you can. Roll them to the bottom of the steps and wait for me." I kissed Henry Mancini and shut him in the cabin for his own safety. The boat was rocking too hard to walk straight, and I wouldn't have him tumbling overboard.

Britta took off on trembling feet as I ran down the corridor to the galley where we cooked and kept the foodstuffs. I yanked a pot out and filled it with all the cups, forks, spoons, knives and dinner plates I could find. I started searching for glass, but my brain was too scattered with equations from Chemistry class; it was hard to think in a straight line. I found a lantern and placed it in my pot of destruction, whipping my head around for other sharp projectiles to toss inside. Bottles, spice containers and cooking utensils were shoved in my pot, and I knew I was running out of time.

I ran on rubbery legs to the bottom of the stairs, where Britta had rolled three barrels while sobbing and shaking. "Good girl! Now, we have to open these and dump out, like a quarter of the cleaner overboard. I'll call Foss through Jamie." Britta was shouting questions at me, but I was concentrating on my link with Jamie. *No matter what you're doing, what I've got down here is more important. Send Foss to me right now!*

Lucy, no! We're barely holding on up here. Stay where you are!

If you don't send Foss down to me, so help me, I'll throw Britta overboard!

You're insane!

Do it now! If I don't see Foss in ten seconds, Britt's going over! I looked up at her apologetically. Of course I would never hurt her, but Jamie wasn't in his right mind enough to call my bluff.

Britta was sobbing as the boat rocked too hard after a heavy bump from the sea monster. The wood groaned, refusing for the moment to splinter. I kissed Britta and sent her back to Henry Mancini, both of us feeling slightly better once she was shut inside with my dog.

A soaking wet Foss came hurtling down the steps with so much rage, I began to question if there was a better person for the job. His eyes were so full of crazy, I nearly peed myself. "I told you to stay in the cabin!" he bellowed above the commotion.

"I can stop the farlig!" I yelled, not understanding how our kiss could have been so explosive, yet he was so mean on a dime.

Foss shoved me against the wall, knocking the wind out of me before relinquishing his grip and letting me fall to the ground. "You don't know what you're talking about."

"I do!" I searched for something he would believe as I clambered to my feet. "It's part of my human magic! I can blow things up. I just need your help. Give me five minutes, and I'll blow a hole clear through its brain!" Before he could argue, I decided to treat him as if he'd already agreed to help. "I need a quarter of the cleaner dumped from those barrels right now!"

Foss snarled at me for good measure and cracked open the tops of the three barrels. In a flash he ran them up the stairs one by one, bringing them back with a mouth ready to yell at me.

"Shut up!" I shouted, unwilling to lose my slight upper hand. "I need more glass. What do we have that's glass or pottery or something that can be broken into sharp pieces?" When he took an entire three seconds to think, I yelled, "Get it now!"

Foss ran up the stairs, and I could hear the men shouting and fighting the tentacles as best they could. Jens's voice boomed out, and terror squeezed me around the throat.

When Foss reappeared with a few more lanterns, I snapped, "Took you long enough! Dump them in the barrels, as much as you can cram in there." He obeyed, looking over his shoulder to the stairwell anxiously. "Focus, Foss!" I clicked my fingers to garner his attention. "This is a bomb we're making. As soon as I add the aluminum from my pot, you've got less than a minute to put the lid back on the barrel and throw the whole thing into the monster's mouth. Can you manage that?"

"Are you kidding me? That's your plan? There's no way you can make a big enough explosion to kill it!"

"Just do it!" I screamed. "One at a time until all three are launched. Everyone else needs to get below deck first. After you throw it, run as fast as you can back down here, or you'll get blasted with shrapnel." When Foss looked like he wanted to question me, I jabbed my finger up the steps. "Go get the others now!"

Jamie! Get everyone down below deck now! Hurry! Foss will help you grab the others.

Foss surprised us both by actually obeying. Mace was the first one down the stairs. He was soaking wet and had a huge gash across his chest. The poor boy was terrified, and nearly collapsed in my arms. "We're not going to make it!" he confessed. His heart clamored against mine.

"We are! I need you to focus, though. Mace, I need your whistle. You have to do something for me."

He looked at me like I was out of my mind, which, to be honest, I pretty much was. He shook his head, and we both knew how incapable he was of focusing right now, but he was also unable to turn me down. "What?"

"We can destroy the farlig, but he has to open his mouth when I say so. Is there a whistle that can make someone open their mouth?"

"Of course, but I'm not strong enough to control something like that!" He flung his hand toward the stairwell as Jamie jumped down to our level.

"What are we doing down here?" Jamie demanded.

"We're killing the sea monster!" I ushered Jamie behind me. "I need you guys to stay here. Mace and Foss can do the work now." When Jamie opened his mouth to argue, I shoved him down the hall. "Just do it!"

Jens and Uncle Rick scrambled down the steps seconds later, with Foss bringing up the rear. Everyone was shouting at me, demanding to know why I was getting them all killed. I responded by pushing Jens and Uncle Rick down the hallway and dragging Mace halfway up the steps, but stopping before our heads breached the surface. "It's to you, Mace. When I say go, give me your best whistle. We don't have many chances to make this happen, so I need you to do your best. We need his mouth open from my command until Foss tosses a barrel in its mouth. I'm counting on you." I looked him in the eye until I was sure he was capable of following the order. When he nodded, I kissed his cheek. "Good boy."

I ducked below deck, counting the men dripping and catching their breath. The wind from the currents was whipping around me, making it hard to think. "Where's Tor?"

Jens shook his head. "He went overboard. He's gone, Loos. So whatever it is you're doing, do it fast. The ship won't hold much longer."

"But dwarves can't swim!" I swallowed my horror after a short bleat of agony passed through my lips. I made quick work of shoving the nightmare into a box until I could properly deal with it, and nodded to Foss. "Hurry, now. Screw on the lid and run to the top as soon as I dump the aluminum in. Aim for his mouth, but don't hold onto the barrel for more than a minute. Toss it at its head far from the boat if it's too close to call, or you'll be the one exploding. Mace! Start your whistle!" I waited until I heard the first note, then I picked up the pot and dumped about a third of the aluminum into the first barrel. "Cover and run, Foss! Launch it and bolt for cover."

Foss's eyes were wide, wondering what I'd gotten him into. Thankfully, he obeyed. The lid in place, he hefted the heavy oak barrel up the stairs past Mace, who kept his whistle strong. My mouth fell open, and unbidden, my feet moved toward the sound.

Jens lunged forward and yanked me back, covering my ears to mute out Mace's lure on me. My brain finally started working again. "Mace, get down here!" I yelled.

Mace's whistle was still going as he backed down the steps. I held onto the two remaining barrels and prayed with everything in me that this worked.

Twenty seconds. Thirty.

Foss charged back down the steps and shoved me against the wall. I wanted to protest, but then I realized as he boxed me in with his massive body that he was shielding me from the blast.

"Stop the whistle, Mace!" I commanded just in time.

I was braced for the explosion, my hands on Foss's heaving chest. The monster's scream, however, no one was prepared for. It was high-pitched and screeched like tires on asphalt.

Foss and I pinned the barrels to the wall as the boat rocked ominously. "Another!" I ordered, motioning for Mace to replay his marvelous whistle. I dumped more aluminum in the barrel, Foss sealed it and charged it up the steps.

Twenty-five seconds. Thirty-five.

Foss's eyes were wide with terror when he returned. "It's working! It's injured for sure."

"Cover your ears!" I warned this time.

The second boom was bigger than the first, and the screaming was gurgled now. The strangled sound was awful and wonderful in equal measure. I hated being the killer, but I could not let my friends and family die like this. The rush it gave me was too unsettling to examine.

"Last one, guys!" I commanded.

Mace poked his head above the stairwell and looked for the monster's head. He came back down. "He's sinking! Hole blown clean through the back of his head! We did it!"

I ran up to the surface and screamed at the carnage. Squid brains were bubbling out of the monster's head. His whole body was sinking slowly, his tentacles unraveling from the boat.

One of the giant black squid arms was thick as a tree trunk and swinging madly in the air like a balloon when you let all the air out. Dread coursed through me as the stickers latched onto the rail and held on as the monster sank, taking the side of the boat with him. "He's not letting go of the boat!" I shouted over my shoulder. "Cut off his arm! Quick, or we'll tip over!"

"Hurry!" Uncle Rick sent the men forward on my order. He began chanting with his eyes closed, using his magic to attempt calming the water. The ocean was far bigger than him, so it did not hearken to his request enough to truly help us.

I plastered my body to the wall as the guys charged up the stairs, slipping and sliding on the lye-soaked surface. I clawed at my face every time one of them fell. Once they landed in the abyss, that would be the end of them.

My eyes fell on a thick rope near the front of the ship. One of the crates had busted open, spilling its contents out on the floor. I don't know what possessed me to run and grab it, but before I knew it, I was sliding across the boat in the darkness, scooping up the rope and tying it to the banister as tight as I could. It was long, and I tossed the end of it clear to the other side of the ship. *Thank you, Dad, for making me play baseball for three summers before you gave in and realized I have little aptitude for sports.*

"Grab on!" I yelled, though my voice could barely be heard above the wind and the chaotic nature of the waves. The only light came from the giant moon, which gave everything a blood red hue. The boat tipped as the sea monster sunk further down, and Foss, Mace and Jamie thankfully grabbed onto the rope to steady themselves. Jens was straddling the railing as he hacked away at the rubbery tentacle, and I sobbed at the mental image of him toppling overboard.

I held tight to the railing and the rope as the boat tipped me higher in the air. My fear of heights combined with my newly discovered fear of sea monsters. I screamed as gravity pulled my body hard toward the farlig's grave.

It was too much. My fingers were slicked with soap, and the water spray from the waves was making everything hard to grip. I saw my life flash in bright bursts before my eyes as both the railing and the rope slipped between my desperate fingers. I prayed a silent plea as I fell for Linus to... make it all better? To catch me?

A strong grip banded around my flailing hand, and I knew in that moment, my brother had heard me.

Twenty-Six.
Mace's Determination

It was not Linus, but it was my brother. I'd fallen all the way across the boat, but did not hit the waves that clawed at me. Mace gripped my arm with wild eyes as I sobbed, feet dangling through the broken rungs of the railing. He hoisted me up, abandoning his post hacking away at the tentacles. Using the rope as a guide, he pulled me to his front.

At this point, I was pretty much useless. I sobbed at the life I'd nearly lost in the sea and clung to his shirt with all I had in me. Using the hand over hand method like he was scaling a mountain, Mace pulled us to the stairwell and deposited me below the deck. I slid down the steps, but was immediately submerged in water.

"No!" Mace cried, jumping down into the darkness and yanking me up. I gasped for air and held onto him as another gust of water threatened to wash me down the hall. "Get on my shoulders!" Mace shouted over the commotion.

I obeyed as quickly as I could with my limbs

trembling. I gripped his neck with my thighs as I pressed my hands to the ceiling of the bottom deck.

No one had thought about all the water collecting below. Uncle Rick was up to his shoulders in water, and Britta held Henry Mancini over her head as the water lapped at her chin.

Uncle Rick was sucking the water into his palms, but he was no match for the steady flow that was streaming down the steps. No sooner would he remove a gallon, then five more would demand being dealt with.

Mace took my hand and placed it atop the back of his palm. Beneath my terror, I felt his hand heat up. Mace closed his eyes and sucked the liquid into his hands at a rate far faster than Uncle Rick.

"No, Charles! That's too fast! You'll hurt yourself!" Uncle Rick called out through the dark tunnel.

Britta whimpered as the water dipped to her shoulders, and she could finally lower her chin.

It was going well until I felt Mace start to shake. I could feel his intensity increasing as the water level fell to his waist. I slid off his rigid body into the pool that only went up to my chest now and took a look at his pinched face.

"Mace, stop!" He had blood trickling down his nose and out of his left ear as he shook with his eyes closed. "No! You can stop!"

"Not... until... you're safe!" he shouted through gritted teeth. Blood from his nose dripped down his chin.

I couldn't take it any longer. I flung myself onto him in a hug that knocked the concentration off his face. He heaved as if breathing for the first time as my friendly attack pushed him up against the wall. "No more," I pled, hoping his love for me would not be the thing that killed him. I buried my face in his soaking chest and let his blood drip down into my hair. "No more."

I had precious little comfort to give him. I was still reliving my almost death and the horror that just looking at the decapitated sea monster inflicted upon me in the oppressive black of the sea. Tor was dead; I would not lose my brother. We hugged each other with weak and shaking arms, clinging to the lifeline with everything left that our adrenaline had not taken from us.

I scooped up a handful of water and washed the blood from his face, fingers trembling when I saw his eyelids droop. "You're okay! You're okay!" I chanted, willing it to be true. "You're okay! You're okay!" I blubbered.

The boat rocked me backwards, pulling him forward onto me as I was submerged underwater. It was even darker underneath the surface in the long hallway, and I fought to keep Mace's heavy body with me as we got turned around with the waves. Flashes of the Nøkkendalig forced out an underwater scream, but I pulled myself together before I lost my head to total panic.

Finally I managed to push us both to the surface. Mace slumped against the wall with his eyes closed, saturated lashes sweeping across his angular cheekbones. I gripped his shirt and held him upright, sobbing as Uncle Rick fought his way through the current to us.

Uncle Rick raised a now unconscious Charles from the pool and breathed in his face. He traced his thumb from Mace's hairline down the slope of his nose, causing a golden symbol with intricate loops and swirls to appear like a glowing tattoo on his forehead.

"That's my boy," Uncle Rick said, letting out a contented sigh when Mace's eyes opened.

I didn't think I would ever stop crying.

Uncle Rick was trying to soothe me while holding his son, but I heard none of it. There simply wasn't time for coddling. "Buckets!" I declared. "We need buckets. This ship's going to sink if we take on much more water. Where are the buckets?"

"There are a few pots and such down the hall in the kitchen. I'll be back." The old man swam down the hall, looking, well, kinda funny doing a breaststroke.

I held Charles upright as he fought to regain himself and process the horror of the moment. Britta waded to us with Henry Mancini and pulled Mace toward the cabin. "Lie on the hammock in here while we work. You can watch Henry Mancini, if you like. I'll help with the buckets.

"No, I..." Mace argued, but he nearly fainted getting out the sentence, so Britta won that one. We supported him and pushed the door open to the cabin. The small room was filled with water up to the hammock, so it was easy to maneuver him up into the netting.

I glanced at the window and noticed the water level was higher than it had been when the terror began. I turned to Britta once Mace was secured in the hammock with my frightened puppy. "Let's form an assembly line for the buckets." We waded back out into the hallway where Uncle Rick was scooping up water near the foot of the steps. "Uncle Rick, can you suck more water in without hurting yourself?" I asked, taking one of the three containers he'd found.

Uncle Rick nodded. "I can. Charles was frightened for you, so he took in too much water at once. I can pace myself."

"Good." I motioned for Britta to go midway up the steps. "We'll use the buckets. You use your magic." I did not wait for a response, only handed a heavy pot to Britta, who ran it to the railing and dumped it over.

"Britta! Get back down there!" I heard Jamie yell. He ran over to her to move her back down the stairs.

"We're flooded down here, Jamie!" I called up to him. "When the monster's gone, send the guys to help us, or we'll take on too much water and sink."

Jamie looked down with wide eyes and saw the water around my chest. "We're coming!" he assured me.

I handed a bucket up to Britta, but the boat rocked, and I fell again. When this was all over, I was never going swimming as long as I lived. I twisted in the water and tried not to have a panic attack when I felt arms around my waist yanking me toward oxygen.

Jens. My perpetual hero and constant safe place. I exhaled in his face and wrapped my arms around his neck as he placed me on the stair. "It's getting too deep for you here." He took my place at the bottom of the stairs and handed up a bucket of water to me. I passed the pail to Britta, who gave it to Jamie to dump overboard, and then Jamie threw it back down the stairs to Jens. With the absence of the squid, the boat did not rock so violently. The assembly line moved like lightning with the extra help, and slowly, very slowly, the water level began to decrease.

Foss steered the ship away from the sight of the fight and on toward safer waters, if such a thing existed.

Twenty-Seven.
The Suck it Up Team

We took turns recouping. Half the group slept and nursed their wounds while the other half of us fought off our exhaustion and tended to the ship. I was on the suck it up team. While Jamie and Britta collapsed in their hammock and cried about Tor and the horror of the night, and Mace and Alrik rested to fend off overusing their magic, I was working.

I took inventory of all the stuff, opening each crate to let the water out. I strung a clothesline across the deck and hung up all the clothes I'd laundered with what was left of the soap. I washed the walls and floors of the bottom deck, then set to scrubbing down the kitchen, washing everything meticulously as my brain short-circuited and went to checkout land. I worked like a madwoman, seeking out mayhem and putting order to it while Foss and Jens repaired damaged parts of the boat as best they could on such limited resources. I worked hard to fend off images of my favorite dwarf sinking like a rock to the bottom of the ocean.

We'd lost a lot in the ordeal, but the food crates were only water damaged, so we would not starve. I cleaned out the last crate and set out the things to dry before I started to swab the deck. The mop had gone missing. Or more realistically, it's possible there never was one aboard. So I got down on my hands and knees and washed the deck with the soap and a rag. It was a huge ship, so I picked a corner and worked my way to the other end, not permitting the tiniest bit to go unpolished. I worked until my knuckles cracked, my fingers bled and my brain fogged over so I didn't have to picture my dead dwarf anymore.

* * * *

I awoke in a hammock, unsure how I got there or for how long I was out. I looked around and judged the hour to be twilight-ish. My once beautiful black nightgown was crusted over with cleaner and ocean crap. It felt so gross on me; I itched to take it off. Mostly because it was also itchy.

I dismounted from the hammock, aching from head to toe. I wondered if this was what it would feel like if I lived to ninety. It was quiet on the main floor, so I tried not to make noise as I unhooked a mostly dry dress from the line and took it down to the bathroom, which consisted of a chamber pot, a steel tub, soap and a small bucket of water. I could hear the others in the galley, eating and recapping about the horrific night. I decided I was not totally ready to be social just yet.

With much care, I washed myself, surprised to find dried blood over cuts I didn't remember acquiring. *Stupid psychic bond.* Then I washed the nightgown that was such a lost cause, I wondered if there was even a point. I had exactly three dresses that fit me and hadn't been tossed overboard, so I couldn't afford to lose one, even if it was torn up. I eyed my blue dress from Elvage, hating that I didn't have access to my jeans and t-shirt because they were stashed somewhere in Jens's bottomless Mary Poppins bag. I took my time drying my hair and cleaning my various scrapes. The one on my lower back Jamie'd earned us stung the most.

When someone knocked on the bathroom door, I jumped. *Please don't be Foss. Please don't be Foss.* "What's up?" I called.

Jamie answered, "I thought you might want these. Clothes from your world."

I cracked the door open, hiding my body behind it. "You're a mind reader, you beautiful man!" I exclaimed, reaching my hand out and snatching at the familiar fabric.

He tapped his forehead and kept his eyes on the ceiling to avoid accidentally seeing something too sexy for his own good. "I actually did read your mind. I'm getting better at it. I know you're running out of clothing."

"Thanks, Jamie." I shut the door and pulled the red Partridge Family t-shirt over my head and slipped on my jeans, loving the feel of comfort that hit me instantaneously. Foss's ring actually matched the shirt, which made me hate it one degree less. "How's Britt?"

I asked, trying to keep my voice light.

"Scared. Sad. Grateful to be alive. Grateful for you."

"Aw, shucks. You say the nicest things." I grabbed the chamber pot and the tub, lifted the push-out window and dumped them overboard. I emerged from the room, clean and more awake. Jamie was spotless, and wearing some of the new clothes I'd bought the guys. "How long have I been asleep?"

"Since Jens found you passed out cleaning the deck." He gave me a look that had a tease and a scold built in. "You know, when we took turns sleeping, it wasn't so that you could do all the cleaning. There was hardly anything left for us to do when we got up."

"Good. That leaves plenty of time for consoling your fiancée. She was nine kinds of scared last night."

"We all were," Jamie agreed. A private smile graced his thicker lips, making him look handsome. "My fiancée. I rather like the sound of that."

"You should. She's a gem."

"But you shouldn't have done all that. We're a team. You're not a servant here."

I walked with him up the steps, carrying my ripped nightgown away from my body so I didn't get wet all over again. "I wanted everyone to rest. It was crazy last night, and I didn't want you to wake up to chores. We lost Tor. You need the space to deal with that." I hung my nightgown on the clothesline, which had been cleared off who knows when.

"And you don't?"

I tapped my temple. "I've got a total breakdown scheduled for five years from now. I'll deal with it then."

"I can't imagine that's healthy."

I shrugged. "I'm always one good cry away from full-on psychotic. Best fend it off for now. Not much time for crazy when there're sea monsters lurking about."

Jamie wrapped his arms around me in a hug I tried not to feel. It was too tender, as if I was fragile and might shatter at the slightest breeze. The worst part was that I did feel on the edge of breaking, so I sucked in my breath and endured the sweetness for four whole seconds before gently extracting myself.

"You saved us last night," he said. "We've been talking about it all day. We wouldn't have survived if it weren't for your human magic explosions."

"Queen Lucy of the Pyrotechnics," I joked. "If I'd remembered my chemistry lessons sooner, Tor might still be alive." Voicing my regret pulled me back into Jamie's arms, as if he thought his embrace might shield me from the public stoning I was sure was coming.

Jamie kissed the top of my head, and instantly I missed my dad. He spoke into my hair, which for some reason relaxed the guilt that was strangling me. "Jens has been beating himself up for not remembering how to do what you did. He sat through most of your classes, so he knew how to make that explosion, but in the heat of it all, it slipped his mind."

"It was a crazy night. I was just talking to Tor about how anxious the sea made him. He liked it better underground." I swallowed. "How long until we reach Elvage? I'm not too wild about the ocean right now, either."

"We're a day and a half out from the port, and then half a week's journey inland. The farlig pushed us a bit off-course. We'll be docking in Bedra."

I kissed Jamie's chest and then pulled away before his kindness could melt me any further. I followed him down the stairs to the hallway that looked completely different in the daylight. There were no traces that the terrifying night even occurred. We went to the end of the hall where everyone was gathered in the galley. I was greeted by the whole group raising their glasses to me. I waved off their toast, red-faced and sat between Jens and Mace as Henry Mancini barked happily at my return to consciousness.

Uncle Rick stood, his glass raised again. "We've not said a proper farewell to Tor or to Nik. I think that should be remedied right now." We raised our glasses as one, united in our grief and guilt-laced relief at barely surviving the farlig. Uncle Rick's voice was clear, his ebony fingers gripping his cup like it needed a good choking. "Though we press on, we remember with heavy and full hearts those who fell by the wayside in the name of our cause. Nik the Man of Valor and Torsten the Mighty, you lived as men and died as heroes, steadfast in your convictions as you fought, even unto death. To Tor and Nik."

We toasted and drank, allowing a minute of silence for reflection. When conversation began to trickle through the somber mood, I turned to my plate.

"Morning, baby. Evening, really. Did you sleep well?" Jens asked, giving me a light kiss. It still made me swoon, and the predictable reaction felt right. Reclaiming enough pieces of normal moments to assemble into a whole life was crucial in the wake of such upset. I kissed him twice for sanity's sake.

I nodded. "Thanks for putting me in the hammock. I didn't realize how tired I was until I passed out."

Jens motioned to my jeans and t-shirt with his biscuit. "I like you looking like you. Don't get me wrong, I love our look on you, too. But there's a charm to your way. I've missed it."

I displayed my t-shirt to him proudly. "Some hot guy got this for me. Total tool, but super hot."

"Hey, now."

Jens passed me some food, and I noticed there were no plates or silverware. "Crap. I blew up all the kitchen stuff. Sorry we don't have anything to eat on, guys."

Uncle Rick smiled at me. "We'll survive. Sacrificing a few creature comforts in exchange for our lives is something you won't hear any complaints about from us. I'm proud of you, my girl."

I blinked up at him in surprise. Heat flooded my cheeks and chest at the sentiment I didn't think I needed to hear from a parent figure until he said it. I looked down and focused on my biscuit. "You guys fought like superheroes. I was down here blubbering like a baby while you were in the thick of it."

Uncle Rick kept his eyes on me. "I'm proud of you, dear."

The back of my neck itched, so I scratched it, still keeping my head bent away from the compliment I wished I didn't crave. "I don't know how you guys did it, hacking off the tentacles and sliding all over the boat. King Arthur level of awesome."

Uncle Rick put down his food and stared me down until everyone else at the table stilled. "Lucy, I'm proud of you."

Tiny tears pricked my eyes, and I swiped at them before they could become a problem. "Thanks, Uncle Rick."

Mace's hand was on my back, and before I knew it, I was in his arms. "I was so scared for you!" I admitted into his shoulder. "You saved my life, and then you almost gave yourself an aneurism trying to rescue us. Are you okay?" I touched his ears, examining his face for signs of permanent damage.

Charles did not pull away from my poking and prodding. Instead he drank me in with those silver-black eyes. "I'm just fine, *kära*. A little tired still, but I plan on remedying that in a little bit."

I kissed his cheeks and pressed my face into his neck. "I'm so glad you're okay. Don't ever do that again."

"Anything you say," he agreed, tangling his fingers in my hair and tugging slightly. The stimulation of my scalp felt so good. I closed my eyes, allowing my head to rest on his shoulder and my soul to quiet from its turmoil.

When my stomach rumbled, I released him, giving Henry Mancini a maternal pat before starting in on my dry biscuit. "Tell me about Bedra," I requested, chewing the dry, tasteless biscuit that crumbled like sand in my mouth. "I don't like not knowing anything about where we're going next."

Jens shifted next to me, and I could tell by the tightness of his jaw and the rigid way he held his body that he did not care for this change in plans.

When no one spoke, Uncle Rick took the lead as if he was about to explain something unpleasant. "Bedra is where the Mare live."

"Like horses? That sounds nice."

"Not horses. It's a land run by women and largely populated by them. Men only pass through or make up a very small percentage if they stay."

Jens shook his head. "We'll travel along the shore. We won't run into any problems with the Mare. No point in talking about it."

Foss leaned back on his bench and rested his shoulders on the wall, a sneer mixing with a smile on his face. "And why wouldn't you want to tell her about the Mare? Seems like you're, I don't know, hiding something, Jens."

Britta moved her hand to her forehead and closed her eyes. "Jens," she scolded. "I thought you stopped getting your lavender powder from the Mare a couple years ago. I thought you got it from the Fossegrimens the last time."

"I do." He shook his head. "I mean, I did back when I was using more heavily. I got it from the Fossegrimens by way of the Mare."

"Oh, Jens." Britta sounded so disappointed in her brother. "What would Mum say?"

"I'm hardly the first guy to get lost there. And if Mum wanted to say something, she wouldn't have left for Be."

Foss eyed my discomfort at the secrets Jens was obviously trying to keep from me. "Would you say you've enjoyed more of the Mare, or more of Lucy?" he jeered.

Uncle Rick cleared his throat. "That's my niece, Foss. She's done nothing to provoke you."

The look of warning Jens gave Foss only made the Grimen's cockiness grow. Jens snarled at the large man. "I made it out in a week. How many times have you gotten lost there? Your people trade with them most often."

Foss linked his fingers behind his head, enjoying the discomfort he was causing. "Oh, I've spent my fair share of time taking in the local flavor. But I don't think my wife cares what I do. You, on the other hand..." Then Foss did something so heinous, my mouth fell open in disgust. He turned and winked at me.

Jens ran his tongue along the edge of his top row of teeth as he seethed. "Call her your wife one more time. Really, I'd love an excuse to beat your face in again."

I scowled at them. I wasn't totally following the conversation, but I did know I was on whatever side of the argument that was not Foss's as a general rule. "Quit trying to get a rise out of him. And me, for that matter. I don't care if he's had girlfriends before me. It'd be weird if he hadn't."

This did not knock the smile off Foss's smug face. "Girlfriends, eh? That's not what I would call them."

I bristled and sat straighter. "Could we talk about something that doesn't make Foss do his evil villain smile? Like Pesta stuffing a soul in a sea monster. That's worth a discussion. Do you think it was one soul, or a whole crapload just jammed up in there?" I used my hands when I talked, not realizing the crudeness of my gesture until it was complete.

Uncle Rick was amused at my terminology. "One is all it takes, no matter the size of the being. But yes, it's troubling that she knew where we were and sent the monster off its usual course to track us."

"How's she finding us?" I asked, hoping for an answer. No one had any idea, which I found unacceptable. "No seriously, guys. How did she find us? In the mountains with that Were, that wasn't a coincidence. And now the sea monster? She's getting more aggressive. Are there any other huge monsters in Undra she could throw at us?"

"Bears," Charles suggested. "But we already know about those. Sleipnir, but we won't be near those till we get to Bedra, and they're pretty rare."

I chewed my powdery biscuit. "What are they?"

"Eight-legged horses that fly. Well, they more like hop really high and far. They couldn't, say, fly across this ocean or a mountain or anything like that." Charles mimed with his biscuit as he spoke, flinging crumbs onto the table.

"Eight-legged horses. Awesome. I really miss normal cats and whatnot from my world." I shot Jens a look of commiseration, but he did not catch it. He was still too busy hiding whatever shame Foss brought up. "Okay, so let's stay on the shore, and maybe we'll steer clear of them altogether."

"We've already established that," Foss complained. "Do you ever say anything useful?"

"How about this one," I began, gearing up to tell him off. It was not Jens's hand on my back, but Mace's that stayed my forthcoming tirade.

"Now, now, sister. Best not let Foss wind you up. We're only halfway done with our mission. There's lots more horrible things he'll be deserving of a good verbal thrashing for. Best pace yourself."

Twenty-Eight.
Sailing for Bedra

Foss steered the ship toward a port that Jens was unhappy with. Jens was edgy about me seeing the Mare, so I didn't pry. It wasn't his secrecy, it was Jamie and Britta that had me on edge. They were unusually quiet around me with cheery you-can-do-it-buddy smiles.

Everyone was packing up the crates to ready for docking except for me. They had categorically refused to let me help because of my manic cleaning bout after the farlig fisk. After I had been laying in my hammock for exactly ten minutes, Foss called me lazy and told me I needed to learn how to steer the ship in case he ever wanted to take a break. He's a real sweetheart. I think just nicely asking didn't even occur to the lunkhead. That's how I ended up next to Foss at the helm of the ship, sitting at his feet and snuggling Henry Mancini. I kissed my dog's fur and rubbed behind his ears, grinning when he ground his head into the touch.

"How long till we dock?" I asked.

"Not too long now. Anxious to meet your boyfriend's little distractions?"

"I know you're being nasty."

"Give the Guldy a prize." He looked off into the distance and adjusted the giant steering wheel. "Now what would make you think that?"

"Because you never talk to me nicely unless your brains get scrambled by fiddle music or you're secretly being terrible."

Foss let a boyish grin sneak out. "Oh, I'm just looking forward to seeing the pedestal you put your boyfriend on get knocked out from under him."

"Careful," I warned. "You almost sound like you care about my relationship. Ipso facto, you care about me. Ouch. That can't feel good, growing a heart from scratch like that. Be careful. Ovaries are next."

He scowled at my joke, so I knew I'd won. "If Jens gets the moonbeams you see in him taken away, it'll crush the both of you. Two lovebirds with one stone."

I felt small, sitting next to his towering form. He had a way of almost convincing me he could be halfway decent, and then reverting back to his predictable wretched behavior. Foss was an open palm you thought might welcome you, but it always managed to slap you instead. And yet, I fell for it every time. My mom would have called that an admirable quality. Linus would have told it like it was: I'm gullible and can't believe anyone's past redemption.

Henry Mancini licked my face, cheering me up from the funk Foss always put me in. I sat on the wood floor, wondering if I would ever feel the urge to get back on a boat after this trip.

"Can I ask you something?" Since it was just us, I felt I could voice my concerns.

"Do you honestly think I could stop you? Go annoy Jamie or his rat."

"Yeah, yeah. You're mean and scary. I get it." I rolled my eyes. "Sit down for a second," I urged, tugging on his pant leg.

Foss grumbled and shook his leg to rid himself of my essence, but complied and sat on the floor, facing me with his back against the ship. He made a big show of how inconvenient I was making life for him, but I could tell he was happy to be off his feet.

"What's the deal with the Mare and Jens?" I asked, rubbing Henry Mancini's fur. He had jumped off my lap and was whining next to me, sounding all kinds of pitiful as he paced in a circle.

Foss scoffed, picking at a thread on his beige pants. "You don't want to hear it. It would ruin the shining image of your precious boyfriend."

"Which is exactly why I'm asking you. You like hurting me, and I'm guessing it's all bad news. So, out with it. Is it an ex? Is that what you were jabbing him about?"

A smug smile crossed his face as he focused on nothing in particular. When his vision narrowed on me, the smile faded. Suddenly, the outright hatred was gone and we were two allies sharing secrets. It was hard to keep up with Foss's mood swings.

"Not one woman so much as a harem. Jens was too popular in Tonttu after he killed those trolls, so he moved around a lot before taking on your family on the Other Side. Many men who spend time in Bedra never come out. Jens made it out, but that's where he acquired his lavender powder addiction. The Mare buy it from my people by the barrel. It's how they keep their men so long." He sighed. "I knew Jens back then. He bought some lavender powder for medicinal reasons. Those trolls messed up his back a little." He shook his head. "It always starts out medicinal. Then a few years later, you're wearing the powder around your neck like a noose."

I nodded, not fully understanding everything. "You know I only got about half of that, right?"

"The tiny size of your brain never surprises me."

Henry Mancini looked up at me with sad eyes and started heaving as he yelped. "Oh, baby! What's wrong? Did you eat something bad?" Foss inched away as my puppy built up a fair amount of sick and barfed it on the deck. My hands were on him in an instant, images of Linus on the floor of the bathroom churning in my rattled psyche.

"Ah!" Foss complained loudly, as if a dog throwing up was the most aggravating thing ever. "Control your wolf, Lucy! We just swabbed the deck."

"I'm the one who cleaned it, you jag. Leave him alone. He's been through a lot."

I trotted down the stairs and fetched a rag made from a ruined garment. I came back to the top and cleaned the spot up, throwing the rag and chunky puke overboard. I crouched next to Henry Mancini and spoke in soothing tones that made Foss groan his annoyance at me. "It's okay, sweetheart. Poor, seasick puppy. We'll be off the boat soon."

Henry Mancini stood on all fours, turned around

in a circle three times, and then collapsed like a dying star.

My chest felt tight until I saw him breathing. "He's okay," I informed Foss, who probably could not have cared less. "What should I do for him?"

"Throw him overboard so he doesn't have to deal with you anymore?" Foss suggested.

I glared at his smirk. "Don't even joke about that. How do I make him get better?"

Foss rolled his eyes at having to care about my problems. "Let me take a look. You're so overly emotional about a simple creature. Jens should never have let you keep this wolf." He looked inside Henry Mancini's mouth and frowned, then checked his fur.

"You shut your smackhole!" I demanded, angry that he was being mean to me while my dog was sick. "Henry Mancini needs me! I'm his family. He came to me, of all people. He knew I would take care of him."

"Fantastic job you've done so far. He looks awful."

I closed my eyes and willed myself not to cry in front of Foss. "Please just tell me what to do. I really can't lose another person I love. I need him to be okay."

Foss's arrogance and snark deflated out of him at my plea. "Get him a dish of water. If it's something he ate, that's the best way to move it through him on the limited cargo we have here."

I ran down the stairs and brought back the water as fast as I could, spilling a little on the way. Foss was bent over my puppy, and I did not like the sight of him so close to something I loved. "Here," I said, handing the wooden bowl with water to Foss.

"Um, Lucy? Back up. Something's wrong."

The concern in his voice sent ice through my veins. "What is it? What did you do?"

Henry Mancini's eyes were shut, and he was growling in his dreamy state.

"Go get Jens right now." His tone was controlled, but I could tell something was very wrong.

I wanted to ask questions, but I obeyed. I ran down to the bottom floor to collect Jens, yanking him from the crate he was packing up. "It's my dog! Something's wrong with him."

Jens wasted no time running to the deck. Foss stood and whispered to Jens while I brought Henry Mancini onto my lap. He was growling at something in his delirious state, but I could not tell what.

Then my sweet puppy did something he had never done before. He turned his head and sank his teeth into my hand, shaking his head back and forth to further rip into my skin. "Ow! No, Henry Mancini! No, no!" I dislodged his jaw from my hand but he came at me again. When he looked up at me with malice I had never before seen on him, my heart froze.

My precious little puppy lunged at me, his gray eyes mutating to a ferocious yellow.

Twenty-Nine.
Henry Mancini

I heard Jamie's cry of surprise from below the deck, and I could tell he was unhappy that I'd let us get bitten.

Henry Mancini barked at me like I was a burglar or something. I held up my hands to remind him who I was. "No, baby! No! It's me! I'm your mama! I love you!"

He lunged at me and bit at my shoe with his maw that was now bubbling with white foam.

Jens was on him in a hot second. He wrestled Henry Mancini until he finally clamped his fangs shut. Henry Mancini struggled mercilessly against Jens to get at me, but fortunately Jens was stronger.

"Loos, Pesta's got him," Jens explained through gritted teeth. "There's nothing we can do for him now."

Horror slammed into me, pushing me forward onto my knees. "No! Don't hurt him! He would never bite me like that. You know he's a good dog, Jens! He didn't mean to do it!"

Jens was a mix of woe, duty, pity and sadness as he looked at me and tried to make me understand. "Lucy, he bit you. Possessed or not, he has to be put down."

"It doesn't even hurt!" I lied as the blood dripped off my shaking fingers onto the floor. "Don't take him away from me! I'll do better! I'll watch him more carefully! I promise!"

"It's got nothing to do with you, honey. Pesta's using him to track us now. He won't stop coming at us till we're all dead." Beneath my panic, I could tell Jens was filled with self-loathing at having to restrain our puppy.

Henry Mancini thrashed in his arms, and I hated the sight of his struggle. "Let him go! I'll hold him. I can calm him down. He needs me!" I reached for Henry Mancini, trying to edge him out of Jens's unyielding grip. "Please, Jens! Stop it! You're scaring him!" I could tell by the pitch of my voice that I was on the verge of bursting into tears as the angst effervesced inside me.

Foss tugged me back, wrapping an arm around my torso like a seatbelt. "Jens, let me do it. She already hates me. You don't want to be the one to end him."

"No." Jens spoke as if he wished it was as simple as someone saving him from the dreaded task. "She's my responsibility. I never should've let her keep a wolf to begin with."

"What's going on up here?" Jamie asked, his hand bloody. Britta, Charles and Uncle Rick came up when they heard the commotion, too, but they all kept a safe distance.

I lunged at Jens when I saw the resolve on his face.

"No, Jens!" I screamed. "I'll do anything! Don't take my dog! Don't murder my puppy! He needs me! You can't give up on someone just because they're a little broken. No!" I scrambled to get out of Foss's grip, but despite my thrashing and frantic movements, Foss's hold on me was as firm as Jens's was on Henry Mancini. My dog and I lunged to get at each other. "I can fix it! I can fix it!"

A solitary tear leaked out of Jens's eye and slid down his cheek. "Baby, he can't be fixed."

"That's what they said about Linus, and those doctors were wrong! *You're* wrong!" I clawed at Foss's arm and threw my entire body weight forward, still short of my destination. "They gave up just because it got hard! He could've been okay! One more round of chemo! You don't know!" I elbowed and kicked at Foss like a madwoman. "Henry Mancini can make it! Just give me a chance! I can make him better! Please, Jens! Please! I'll think of something! Just give me some time!"

Foss grew frustrated with me almost escaping from his grip, so he pinned my front to the floor with his obnoxiously large body, crushing half the air from my lungs. "I can do it, Jens. Really," Foss offered, face grim.

"No. He's half mine. My responsibility." Jens took a long, hard look at the beast that was no longer Henry Mancini, ignoring my shrieks. I screamed and clawed at the floor to move closer to them, but Foss was too heavy on top of my back. "Don't look, baby."

Foss covered my eyes with his too-large hand, but the sound was clear as day. Swish, yelp and pop, followed by the sound of Henry Mancini's last breath escaping his tiny lungs in a whimper.

"Linus!" I screamed, sobbing like the mess I was.

Foss scraped me off the deck, rolled me over and brought me to his chest in a hug I was too distraught to examine the oddity of. He picked me up and carried me past the gawkers down to the room he'd taken as his. He said not one disparaging word as he sank to the floor with me on his lap. He was a hoarder guarding the treasure he hated.

I punched his chest as I cried.

"Go on. Let it out."

My ineffectual fists did not damage him as I hoped they would. He'd restrained me and kept me from saving my dog. Henry Mancini was gone, and Foss would pay the price. I wailed on him, refusing to be softened by his arms around me. My knees gripped his hips as I sobbed.

Foss waited out my fury with patience, breathing deeply when my punches turned to girlish slaps across his hard face. "That's it," he soothed me. "I know. It's been a hard life."

I hated that he was the sane one in this moment. The one time I needed him to be more horrible than me, and he let me down. I slapped him once more before collapsing in his arms like a rag doll. I buried my face in his neck and alternated between crying and screaming, knowing that no matter how many friends I made, I would always be alone.

Love *Fossegrim*? Leave a review!

Enjoy a free preview of *Elvage*,
Book four in the Undraland Series

One.
Stargazing with Foss

"He's been gone too many days, Alrik," Foss complained, leaning back against the boat's rail. "We should never have sent Jens to Bedra without a chaperone."

"Patience, friend," Alrik answered, his gray beard outlining his tight smile. "I've never known Jens to fail. He wouldn't stand for it. Too stubborn."

I'd bitten my nails too often for them to appear ladylike. I'd lost my twin brother, my parents, Nik, Tor and Henry Mancini. And now Jens was taking his sweet time coming back to us. He was supposed to be gone one night, but that was a week ago. Jens had been sent to secure horses for us to travel on, plus more supplies since a lot of ours were washed overboard when the farlig fisk attacked Foss's ship.

Well, it was my ship, technically. Since Foss had been declared dead, I inherited all his possessions due to our sham marriage. Foss and I did not agree on much, but we worked together surprisingly well on the boat. He would show me how to fix a leak or clean a part of it, and I pretty much did whatever he asked.

While the others lounged and planned, Foss and I worked until we were exhausted at the day's end. I did anything to occupy my mind so it did not dwell on the very real possibility that Jens was next on the list of people I loved that were now six feet under.

"Not like that," Foss said, correcting the back and forth hand movement I was using to scrub the walls. "You need to go in a circle, or it won't be even. Everyone knows that."

"Sorry. Like this?" I changed my scrubbing accordingly.

"Is it in a circle?" he asked.

"Yup."

"Then that's how I want it."

If I was new to Foss's "cheery" nature, his constant negativity and criticism would have been tiresome. But having grown used to his personality, I did not take offense. I was too concerned with Jens's prolonged disappearance to properly argue with Foss.

This seemed to be the only thing that softened the brute. That, and my brother Charles Mace had done his freaky Huldra whistle a few more times to strip away bits of the curse that kept Foss the surly jerk he was. That had been a long night of Foss puking overboard while I held him. Since his last stripping two nights ago, he was noticeably less argumentative.

"Do you want me to start over? I can do it all again with your circle swipes on the deck." I had maybe three feet left to wash on the entire ship, but it didn't faze me. I wanted the distraction.

Foss examined my work and shook his head. "No. Just remember for next time."

"Okay." I finished up and threw my rag in the bucket. I was sweating from head to toe, but didn't care. It's not like I was gunning for a beauty pageant or anything. My jeans had seen better days, and my purple tank top had dirt and blood stains on it from our various adventures. I stood and stretched my arms over my head, twisting my waist to get some feeling back in my body. "What's next, boss?"

It was rare I surprised Foss, but the shirtless hulk of a man looked at me like I'd just started speaking in French. "It's almost dark."

"You can go to sleep, but I'm not tired. What else needs to be done?"

He looked around, casting for things we'd not tackled. "Nothing really. A few things we'll need daylight for. Repairing nets is impossible in the dark."

"I've got good eyes. Show me how," I demanded. The others were eating in the galley, but I had no interest in socializing or eating more of the stale, powdery biscuits. There was a tin of random-meat jerky left, but honestly, I'd rather chew on the dirty rag I'd just cleaned the boat with.

"Everyone else is eating," Foss pointed out.

"Oh. Go ahead. You must be starving." I rubbed the back of my neck. Though it had been a couple weeks since my long blonde hair had been lopped off to an inch below my chin, it still felt strange to have the wind touch my neck. "Where are the nets? I'm sure I can figure out how to fix them."

"Take a break, little rat." He mussed my filthy hair with something that almost resembled affection. "Rat" used to be strictly derogatory. After we survived

Fossegrim together, there was less hatred in his dealings with me.

"Nets?" I asked again. If I stopped, everything would come crashing down on me. The deaths, the fear... and Jens.

To be clear, it wasn't that I missed my boyfriend, which of course, I did. The thing that kept my hands working was the thought that he would never come back, which was a very real possibility.

Foss gave me a hard look, and then led the way to one of the rooms below deck. He yanked out giant rope nets that weighed at least triple one soaking wet me. He hauled them up to the deck so we could take advantage of what was left of the dipping sun. Opening the bundle up on the wood floor, he pointed to a frayed edge. "See that? It needs fixing. And this?" He showed me a severed knot. "Retying would do the trick." He brought up a box filled with supplies I would need. "But it can all wait until tomorrow. I was going to do it anyway. We're running low on food, so I was planning on taking the boat out a little ways to catch some fish."

"You're giving up on Jens coming back," I stated flatly, fingering the edge of the net.

Foss rolled his eyes. "You're so dramatic. The Mare won't kill Jens. They'll just... detain him. He's fine. Taking his sweet time, but fine. I'm not giving up. I'm catching dinner so we can eat while he wastes our time."

"Okay." I nodded, sitting down on the deck and pulling the net onto my lap. "Go on down and eat something."

Foss looked like he wanted to argue, but left

anyway. As much as I loved when he was gone, his absence left me alone with my thoughts, and my thoughts these days were pretty grim. I couldn't shake the memory of my rabid dog snapping to get at me from Jens's arms, and the awful sound he made when Jens killed him.

Images of Jens with an arrow through his chest flooded my brain before I could stop them. Jens with a knife in the back. Jens on a guillotine. Jens beaten up and left rotting in a ditch. He was Superman to me. Something about the feel of waiting in angst for your protector to return can make a girl nuts. Nuts enough to clean an entire pirate ship.

I did a thorough job with the nets, going through each little notch, inspecting it for any signs of weakness, and repairing the parts when I saw fit. It was the perfect task – never-ending.

The others ate and turned in for the night. Britta and Jamie hugged me, looking only mildly concerned for Jens's welfare. Jamie treated the whole thing like an annoyance, as if Jens was purposefully being detained. Britta was not as concerned as I thought a sister should be, but I took her gentle strength as a rubric for how freaked out I would allow myself to be on the outside. On the inside, I would go nuts and bolts. To the world, I would quietly tie knots in a fishing net alone in the corner on my dead husband's ship. Totally emotionally balanced.

Alrik gave me a kiss on the top of my head, and Charles hugged me before poking me in the side with his prehensile tail to provoke a tease out of me. He earned a simple smile, which he seemed satisfied with, thank goodness.

With everyone tucked in their hammocks down below, I sat in the red moonlight with the repair kit as I looped and knotted.

"Would you stop it?!" Foss cried from across the deck. I could see his neck muscles tensed even in the light of Undra's giant moon.

I stilled, turning to him. "What?"

"The rocking you do. It's deranged! Just go to bed. You'll send me over the edge if you keep this up."

"What rocking?"

Foss smacked his forehead. "You don't even know you're doing it! You were rocking back and forth like a madwoman. Go to sleep, Lucy. We're docked. There's no reason for you to work like this."

"Am I being loud?" I snapped.

"No. You barely run your mouth anymore."

"Am I in the way over here in the corner, or when I was cleaning the boat with you all day?"

"No."

"Then shut up about it. I'm not hurting anyone. Go to bed. You're starting to get crabby all over again. Don't make me call Mace up here to strip that curse off you again."

Foss stomped back down the stairs, resurfacing minutes later with a biscuit and bit of beef leather. Delish. He shoved the food scraps at me. "Here. Eat."

"Oh. Thanks." I took the food and eyed him with the signature skepticism we regarded each other with. "Why are you being nice?"

"I'm not allowed to be nice?"

"I don't trust it." I sniffed the biscuit for signs of

poisoning. He rolled his eyes at my skepticism as he sat down a few feet from me. I took in his less than aggressive demeanor and shifted my attitude accordingly. "Aren't you tired?"

"Exhausted," he admitted, surprising both of us with his honesty. "I'm not looking forward to the trek back to Elvage. Circhos roams the forest. He's more of a pain than you, if you can imagine. I'm not sure how Alrik's planning on getting close enough to the portal to destroy it. Security was pretty heavy when we left."

I thought back on our failed attempt. "I never really worry about the plan when Uncle Rick's on it. I don't really need to see how the rabbit comes out of the hat. I just enjoy the show and clap when I'm told."

Foss gave a companionable snort. "You know, I think I'm around you too much. I actually understood that." He leaned against the side of the boat and folded his hands behind his head. "He's fine, you know."

My fingers slipped on the knot I was retying. "Yup."

"You should get some sleep. Tomorrow I'll teach you how to catch fish with the nets. You'll like it, but you'll need your strength."

I nodded, taking in his big brotherly words curiously. I took a bite of the biscuit and swore off disgusting sand bread as soon as proper food reentered our lives. "Look. This whole you being nice thing is great, but I keep expecting an anvil to fall on my head or something. Why the sudden change?"

Foss did not look at me as he spoke, but cast his eyes up to the stars that were sparkling next to the giant moon I knew I would never get used to. He sighed. "It's my ring around your neck."

I looked down at the heavy gold ring and giant ruby stone with his crest emblazoned on the sides. "Oh. I told you that you could have it back. I don't have to wear it if it bothers you."

"No. Keep it. It's one of the few things I've done that I'm actually a little proud of."

"Huh. I thought you hated me."

Foss grinned, scratching his bare chest. "Oh, make no mistake. I wish you were anyone else."

I pointed to his heart. "That's my darling husband."

"But you were in a tough spot. I'm glad I stepped up and paid Jens back by speaking for you."

"I really hate that term."

"Why do you think I keep using it?" He aimed his smile at me, and I could tell there was a tease behind the mean words. Foss was actually being playful. Huh.

"Well, I appreciate it."

He eyed the ring with a faraway expression. "I swore if I ever did marry, I'd treat my wife like a queen."

I scoffed. "You hate women. You hate me. What makes you think a ring would magically change all that?"

"It's just not how I pictured it. I don't really know what to do with you."

"Nothing. Do nothing with me. I don't need to be handled. You're being fine. Teach me how to work our boat."

"My boat."

"Technically, it's mine, but I'll let you think it's still

half yours."

"And we're back to hate," he joked. "You need to sleep."

"I had a dad, and he stopped telling me when to go to sleep at like, seven. I have a boyfriend who treats me like an adult most of the time. Who do you suppose you are that you get to tell me what to do?"

With a solemn face, he answered, "I'm your husband."

I laughed. I couldn't help it. He was just so sincere. My hand tapped my heart to let him know that he touched something tender and cute. "Oh, darling husband, you're in for such a surprise when we get to my world."

"You need to sleep," he repeated, gently taking the net away from me. "Jens will come back. Punishing yourself like this isn't going to bring him home any sooner."

I had nothing to say to this. He was right, and what was more confusing, he decided to be a decent guy for once. That, coupled with malnutrition and sleeplessness, made for a lapse in my smart retorts. "I, um, I guess you're right." I muscled my way through the rest of my biscuit. "Thanks. You know, you're not a complete tool every now and then."

"Thank you?" he said with half a smirk. He tilted his head back and pointed to the charcoal sky. "Sleeping under the stars again?"

Since he was attempting polite conversation, I decided to take a chance and ride that train. The worst he could do was push me off it. Again. "Yeah. Doesn't feel right sleeping in the hammock without Jens or

Henry Mancini."

Foss slid down so he was lying supine on the floor. He jerked his chin to the empty spot next to him. "Come take a break."

I eyed the spot warily, checking it for booby traps before settling down next to him. "You know, Jamie'll feel it if you dump my body overboard. Built-in security detail."

He chuckled and pointed to a cluster of stars overhead. "That's *Orwandil.* It means bad fortune, and it settled right in the middle of the sea. It's usually closer to Bedra." He pulled me closer so our sides were touching. "I should've looked at that before we shoved off. Might have given us a decent warning."

His skin was cool to the touch, so I rubbed his stomach to warm it, smiling a little when I could tell I'd hit a ticklish spot. "It just looks like a mess of lights to me. How can you tell what's what?"

"Years of practice. That one's my star." He was singling one out in the sky, but I couldn't separate the lights. "Everyone in Undra has a star that tells their story. It moves with them."

"Seriously? Are you just making this up to see how gullible I am? Because I'm pretty tired and would believe almost anything at this point."

He glanced at me as if I was an idiot. "Of course it's true. There I am, right above us." He moved his eyes back up to the heavens. "And if you're tired, you should go to sleep."

"Then why would Olaf believe you're dead? He can just look up and see which star's yours."

Foss cracked a modest smile as he spoke. One of

his arms reached over his torso and brushed against my fingers, touching the tips like little kisses as he directed our hands to his navel. "Stars aren't something educated people put a lot of hope in. Most write it all off as myth, but my mother knew better. She taught me how to find people's stars and use them for tracking. I can predict the weather, hunting trends, tide flow – lots of things just by looking up at the stars. It's not always clear, but sometimes the sky speaks to me."

"You're totally serious right now." I was amazed that he indulged in something so poetic. "You know, if we get over to the Other Side, you have to try this out on a girl. It's a pretty good line. Very romantic."

"It's not a line. It's the truth." He motioned up to a tiny star that kept sparking from dull to super bright. "That one's you. I noticed the change in the sky the night you crossed over. See how it flickers? The more violent the swing, the worse your state is. It's how I knew you weren't doing so well tonight."

My mouth dropped open. "Are you serious? That one there? That's me?" My voice quieted, and I could hear the ocean gently lapping at the boat. "I have my very own star?"

"You do. No matter where you go, I can always find you using your star." His other hand wound through my hair, twirling around the curls as if we had no cares in the world at all.

"That's... that's pretty cool, Foss."

"Watch that one there. The bright one to the left."

I rolled onto my side, and snuggled up next to the meanest man I'd ever been forced to work with, marveling at both the star and the oddity of life's wild waves. "It's pretty," I commented. No sooner had the words escaped me did the star blink and shoot across the sky. "Whoa! Did you see that? How did you know it was going to do that?"

"Lots of nights on this boat. I told you. My mother taught me well. I'm the only one of the four powers that started off as a slave. The others dismiss the stars, but it's how I was able to build up my kingdom."

"Hey," I said, changing the subject. "I bought you something when you sent me shopping before we left."

"Did you buy me a real wife?" he teased, picking up my fingers that were tangled through his so he could examine them.

"Ha. No, I bought you a fiddle. I know you don't play anymore, but in case you wanted the option, I wanted you to have it. Went overboard, though."

Foss was quiet for an entire minute before speaking. "I don't play anymore." His words and tone were finite, so I knew not to push him.

I was familiar with the loss of a desire to play. I recall being a lot more fun before Linus died. I took a chance and leaned up, pressing a light kiss to Foss's temple to acknowledge whatever pain he'd gone through to get him to the point in life where play was not an option anymore.

Foss turned his head and pushed his lips to my forehead, holding me there a few beats as he breathed into my skin with his eyes closed. "For what it's worth, you're not the worst wife a man could have."

I don't know why I took his bitter words as a sincere compliment, but I draped my arm around his chest, holding him as strangely as he held me. I didn't understand our dynamic, but I was too tired to run from it anymore that night.

Though my shoulder was uncomfortable on the flat hard surface, my body relaxed at the first promise that I'd decided to stop working it to death. Exhaustion flooded my senses, and I yawned into his neck as Foss told me stories about different adventures he'd had on this very ship. He sounded like a pirate as he talked about searching out different islands for various resources, and which ones had the easiest locals to trade with.

I'm pretty sure I muttered "goodnight" or something to that affect before I succumbed to my body's wailing for a night of rest. Whatever strange twist of fate landed me under the stars lying with my temple pressed to Foss's neck, I decided not to question it. I welcomed the small amounts of peace I could grasp at and fell into a deep sleep as the waves rocked us with their gentle caress.

Read *Elvage*,
the next book in the series

Join my newsletter and view my other books at
www.maryetwomey.com

Other books by Mary E. Twomey

The Saga of the Spheres
The Silence of Lir
Secrets
The Sword
Sacrifice

The Volumes of the Vemreaux
The Way
The Truth
The Lie

Jack and Yani Love Harry Potter

Undraland
Undraland
Nøkken
Fossegrim
Elvage
The Other Side

Undraland: Blood Novels
Lucy at Peace
Lucy at War
Lucy at Last
Linus at Large

Find your next great read and sign up for the
newsletter at www.maryetwomey.com

DATE DUE

Made in the USA
San Bernardino, CA
20 December 2017